"We could pretend
to be madly in love."

"My grandfather would never believe that," she asserted coolly.

"He'd be shocked, but I think we could convince him." Brendon smiled lazily, and his eyes danced with devilish confidence. "That is, if you want the presidency as much as you say you do."

"I want it," she confirmed with soft defiance. "How do you suggest we get our point across?"

Brendon waved his hand. "Passionate glances, whispered endearments, the soft touch of my hands on your shoulder. Come on, Savannah, use your imagination. You're going to have to make him think you're serious about 'the worst scoundrel in the state.'"

"That's wicked," she accused, warming to his roguish grin.

"It will work," he emphasized calmly.

Dear Reader:

The event we've all been waiting for has finally arrived! The publishers of SECOND CHANCE AT LOVE are delighted to announce the arrival of TO HAVE AND TO HOLD. Here is the line of romances so many of you have been asking for. Here are the stories that take romance fiction into the thrilling new realm of married love.

TO HAVE AND TO HOLD is the first and only romance series that portrays the joys and heartaches of marriage. Its unique concept makes it significantly different from the other lines now available to you. It conforms to a standard of high quality set and maintained by SECOND CHANCE AT LOVE. And, of course, it offers all the compelling romance, exciting sensuality, and heartwarming entertainment you expect in your romance reading.

We think you'll love TO HAVE AND TO HOLD romances—and that you'll become the kind of loyal reader who is making SECOND CHANCE AT LOVE an ever-increasing success. Look for four TO HAVE AND TO HOLD romances in October and three each month thereafter, as well as six SECOND CHANCE AT LOVE romances each and every month. We hope you'll read and enjoy them all. And please keep your letters coming! Your opinion is of the utmost importance to us.

Warm wishes,

Ellen Edwards

Ellen Edwards
SECOND CHANCE AT LOVE
The Berkley Publishing Group
200 Madison Avenue
New York, N.Y. 10016

Second Chance at Love®

INTIMATE SCOUNDRELS
CATHY THACKER

A
**SECOND CHANCE AT LOVE
BOOK**

To Mom and Dad

For all the hours you've listened to,
counseled, and guided me;
and for being there
when I needed you most.

CHAPTER
One

SAVANNAH MCLEAN GLANCED in exasperation at the groups
of well-dressed businessmen and women who were dining
in the elegant Barbados Room of the Mills House Hotel.
Fragrant camellias adorned every table. The clink of silver
and china rose above the low hum of voices and subdued
laughter. She scowled back at her grandfather.

"Stop acting as if I had assigned you a fate worse than
death!" he demanded, unfolding a white linen napkin across
his lap. "I simply want you to date a few trustworthy, eligible men."

Savannah leaned back in her chair. Shaking her shoulder-
length ebony curls, she couldn't resist teasing. "No rakehells
or rogues, Grandfather? Just reliable types?"

Emerson gave her a dour look over the rim of his bifocals.
"I expect you to use common sense when selecting your
beaux. I'm trying to improve your social life, my dear, not
destroy you."

Savannah loved her grandfather dearly. She felt proud to have inherited his formidable strength and determination as well as his brilliant blue eyes. But that didn't mean she would allow him to interfere in her personal life. "You're trying to get me married again," she said. "It won't work. I'm a free woman and I intend to stay that way."

Making no effort to mask his disappointment, Emerson regarded her seriously. "For how long?"

"The rest of my life." Her words were tinged with bitter resolve.

"Savannah, a divorce isn't the end of the world," Emerson argued, his tone softening.

"It was for me. Now that my life is back to normal, I refuse to complicate it unnecessarily again. Besides, who needs a man?" She gestured effusively. "All they're good for is—"

"Savannah!" her grandfather interrupted, his face scarlet.

"Taking out the garbage and . . ." She grinned mischievously. "Fooled you, didn't I?"

Emerson sighed. "My dear, there are times when you really do make me feel my age." He straightened and took another sip of bourbon. "However, it's time you stopped blaming yourself for the divorce," he lectured sternly. Their eyes met. "Your marriage failed because you chose the wrong man. Had you stayed here in Charleston and married someone of whom I approved instead of running off to California to make your fortune in the booming real estate market there, the results would have been different."

Would they? She wondered. She and Keith had loved one another deeply. At first life had seemed so perfect. They'd had each other; they'd had their careers. She sold real estate during the day and worked on her MBA at night. Keith had been a junior partner in a struggling law firm, and though he lost nearly as many cases as he won, he'd had high hopes for the future. Then Savannah's career had taken off. Keith began to resent her success, and nothing was the same again. "I'm not ready to date yet," she said quietly.

"Then you'd better start preparing yourself, because I

have no intention of allowing you to turn into an old maid," Emerson countered calmly, slicing into his filet mignon.

Savannah rolled her eyes and put down her spoon, pushing her bowl of she-crab soup to the side. "Grandfather, you can be positively medieval at times!"

"And proud of it," Emerson affirmed.

Shaking her head, Savannah gazed restlessly around the room. Immediately she noted a handsome executive dining alone several tables away. With effort she forced her attention back to her meal. Just because the man was attractive was no reason to stare.

"I don't care how much you protest, Savannah," Emerson continued valiantly. "I'm going to welcome you home in style. Now that you're settled in, I'd like to throw a party in your honor."

Savannah put down her coffee cup. "Oh no, Grandfather. Please. I know you mean well, but I'm really not up to it. I've got my career now, and for the moment that's more than enough. Maybe later."

Emerson stared at her in vexation. Again she gazed around the restaurant, noticing the same devastating young executive. He was wearing navy blue dress slacks that were pleated slightly at the trim waist. His shoulders and chest filled his light blue blazer with ease. His trim form was accentuated by a crisp navy and powder blue pinstripe-on-white shirt. She estimated him to be somewhere in his early thirties.

Apparently he, too, had finished his meal. He'd pushed back his chair and propped one ankle casually over the other knee. A stack of white papers was piled in front of him, and he held a ball-point pen in his right hand. Thoroughly oblivious to his surroundings, he read, scribbled, read, frowned, and scribbled even more vigorously. Savannah smiled, thinking how often she, too, had worked through meals.

Dreamily she studied the man's medium-length brown hair, which was as wildly curling as her own. His nose was straight and well proportioned, his cheekbones high. His lips were full yet undeniably masculine. When his mouth opened, his teeth flashed a dazzling white.

As if noticing her prolonged perusal, the stranger abruptly raised his head, quirked his brows, and flashed a flirtatious grin. Heat stealing into her cheeks, Savannah turned hastily back to her grandfather.

"Interesting crowd here today, isn't it?" Emerson commented. "See anyone you'd like to say hello to?"

"Actually I think I'll dash to the powder room." Feeling a sudden need to escape the stranger's undeniable stare, Savannah rummaged under the table for her purse.

"Take your time." Emerson stood and gallantly held her chair. "I've got a few cronies I'd like to talk to on the other side of the dining room. Unless you'd like me to wait and introduce you." He raised a speculative brow and withdrew an imported cigar from his pocket.

The man was still watching her, his expression slightly perplexed. Catching her eye, he smiled and stood too, tossing his napkin aside. Savannah gulped as a nameless emotion tautened her middle. She knew she wasn't ready for a close encounter with this man. The scars from her divorce were still too new.

"Some other time, perhaps, grandfather." She tucked her clutch under her arm and strode rapidly away, feeling incredibly foolish as she ducked into the powder room. She was a grown woman, not a child! Why had she acted as if the delectable stranger were a threat?

She brushed her hair into sophisticated waves, applied lip gloss, and checked her blush, unaccountably reluctant to rejoin her grandfather. She adjusted the ascot tie on her white silk blouse, smoothed the sleek lines of her chinaberry skirt into place, and tugged down the matching suit jacket. When at last she could think of no reason to delay further, she strode through the paneled hall, intending to make her excuses to her grandfather and return to the office.

"Excuse me, miss," a low voice said at her shoulder. "I believe you dropped this."

She turned to find herself face to face with the handsome stranger. He held a white handkerchief in his hand and was studying her with sable brown eyes.

"It's not mine," she managed to say coolly.

"Sorry I bothered you then." He slipped the square of white cotton casually into his pocket and started to walk away. But when he'd gone only two steps, he turned back to her. He gazed at her appreciatively, his stance lazy and relaxed.

Perspiration dampened her palms; her heart thudded. For months she had avoided men. She'd needed to make a fresh start in her career, needed to become accustomed to living alone again. But with one raking glance, this man made her remember what it was like to be infatuated. He also made her acutely aware of how alone she had been. The realization stung.

"You're new in town, aren't you?" His brows knitting together, he took another step forward.

Damn you, Savannah thought. I was doing just fine without you! "Yes."

"I thought so. Charleston's a small town." His thumb and index finger idly traced his jaw. "I know I would have remembered, had we been introduced."

"I'm sorry if I appeared to be watching you during the meal," she said politely.

He laughed. The sound was low, vibrant, and intensely masculine. "As it happens, I never hold anything against a beautiful woman." Before she could stop him, he had captured her right hand and was pressing it against his warm lips. She was too stunned to move.

"You've been watching too many old movies," she bantered, struggling for composure. Blood pounded in her head. A thousand forgotten feelings fluttered in her middle. "No gentleman kisses the back of a woman's hand anymore, not even in South Carolina."

"I found it a delightful experience," he told her, teasing glints shining in his eyes. "What do you say we throw caution to the winds and exchange names?"

Without thinking she gave him a tight, dismissing smile. "I don't think so." She began to move away, but he reached out to grab her hand and turn her back to him. He stared at her for a long moment. "If I've offended you . . ."

"You haven't."

His brow arched. His full mouth thinned.

Savannah cleared her throat. Warmth radiated from the light grasp he held on her wrist. "Apparently I gave you the wrong impression."

"I want to get to know you," he said calmly. "What's wrong with that?"

"Nothing, under socially correct circumstances," she replied, aware of people turning to watch their low exchange. She fought a cringe of embarrassment. "Please, I've got to go."

"You mean if we'd met at a party and a pillar of local society had stood up and made the introductions, it would be all right. We could converse." Mockery laced his tone. Realizing how ridiculous she'd sounded, heat flooded her face.

Just then her grandfather rounded the corner and stopped dead in his tracks, anger reddening his features. "Sir, I'll thank you to get your hands off my granddaughter this instant!"

Savannah widened her eyes in surprise. Her grandfather rarely lost his temper in public.

Patrons at the coat check turned to better take in the contentious scene, but that didn't stop Emerson in the least. He went on more fiercely than before. "You can see you're upsetting Savannah! Why, she's as white as a sheet! And unless I miss my guess, you're the one who was distracting her all during lunch! Why, the poor woman had to flee from the room to get away from your lecherous stare! And here you are bothering her again!"

Savannah was mortified. "Grandfather, please, don't say another word," she begged hoarsely. "You've completely misinterpreted the situation. He didn't—"

"Savannah, don't tell me you encouraged this gentleman!" Emerson exclaimed.

Guilty heat flooded her cheeks. She floundered. The stranger stepped in kindly. "Let me explain."

"The devil you will!" Emerson shot back. His hand protectively circling Savannah's elbow, he held her close to his side. "I know who this scoundrel is, honey, even if you don't." He fixed the man with a meaningful glare. "And if you ever so much as come within ten feet of my grand-daughter again, I'll have you run clear out of Charleston! Is that clear?"

The man shook his head as if to clear it. "Sir, I don't know what you think has been going on here, but..." He took a deep breath and glanced at Savannah as if for help.

She melted like ice cream on a warm day. Dear heaven, he was compelling! Maybe her grandfather was right. Maybe she had been out of circulation too long. "Grandfather, please calm down and explain yourself. And why did you call him a scoundrel?"

"Because he is—one of the worst this state has ever seen."

The tall man smiled and surveyed Emerson with an insolent gaze before turning to Savannah with easy charm. "Forgive me for not introducing myself sooner," he said. "I'm Brendon Sloane, owner of Sloane Construction." She found her hand clasped firmly in his. The sensual warmth of his touch traveled all the way to her toes. Slowly he released her, but her hand continued to prickle with sensation.

Her legs were shaky, but her tone was composed. "Sloane Construction. That's McLean Development's chief rival."

Brendon nodded. "That's correct, and you must be the heir who's come to take over your grandfather's firm."

"I'll be retiring in April," Emerson acknowledged stiffly, "but my successor has not yet been named." He turned grimly back to Savannah. "If you were to take over the presidency of McLean Development, Savannah, this is the kind of snake in the grass you'd be up against. It would be one zero hour after another, with no guarantee that a gentleman's code of ethics would be observed."

Brendon laughed deep and low in his throat. Savannah noticed he wasn't denying anything Emerson had asserted. "Stay away from my granddaughter, Mr. Sloane," Emerson warned. "And Savannah, you stay away from him too!"

As Emerson led her out of the lounge, past the front desk of the restaurant, and through the marbled lobby, she felt Brendon's gaze still on her. It wasn't an easy sensation to shake off or forget.

CHAPTER
Two

DURING THE RIDE back to McLean Development's downtown office, Emerson steadfastly refused to discuss Brendon Sloane or his own dislike of the man. He simply reiterated his request that Savannah stay as far from him as possible. "I want you to get back into circulation socially," Emerson reiterated, "not sink to the depths."

"And you think that's where a liaison with Brendon would take me?" Savannah teased, recalling the pang of longing she'd felt when he'd kissed her hand.

"Sloane is a shrewd businessman, but he's never been accepted by society here. He can be ruthless when it comes to getting what he wants. I don't want you involved with him," Emerson stated grimly.

Savannah sighed, disturbed by his pique. "He seemed a gentleman until you came along."

"That's just it. Sloane would be a gentleman until you crossed him." Emerson directed his car into the parking space bearing his name. Adroitly he changed the subject. "By the way, how is your evaluation of the Edisto Island project coming?"

"I should have something ready to present tomorrow." She hoped her report would firmly establish her expertise in marketing and innovative development. Emerson strolled with her into the building. "I'm sure you'll do fine, Savannah." He patted her shoulder reassuringly. "Certainly you've put in enough hours on it. You've only been back six weeks, but you're as familiar with company operations as if you'd worked here for years."

"Thanks." She grinned. "Now that you realize my worth, maybe you'll keep me in mind for the company presidency."

They parted at the elevator. Savannah spent the rest of the afternoon in her office going over the final costs, proposed sales presentations, and blueprints of the many floor plans for the Edisto Island Project. Emerson dropped by at about five, an all-weather coat draped over one arm. "Still working, I see?" he asked affectionately.

She looked up from the stack of papers on her desk. "Mmmhmm."

"How about having dinner with me tonight at the Wine Cellar on Prioleau Street?"

She glanced at her watch and ran a hand through her hair. Her spine ached from the hours she'd spent hunched over her desk, and the beginning of an eyestrain headache throbbed in her temples. "I'd like to, but I've still got an awful lot to do here."

Emerson frowned. "Savannah, I know you want to prove yourself, and you've made an admirable start, but no one expects you to stay late every night. I want you to go out and have a little fun."

She stretched in her chair, soothing the crick in her neck. "The Edisto Island Project has problems."

"We'll discuss them tomorrow," Emerson decided. "Now how about dinner? Are we on or off?"

The thought of another evening alone did not appeal to her. Her stomach growled hungrily to second the motion. "On," she decided cheerfully.

"Great." Emerson beamed down at her. "I'll meet you at the restaurant. Right now I've got to run these new cost estimates over to the school board."

True to her word, Savannah arrived at the elegant restaurant at six twenty-five. The parking lot was jammed, and the restaurant was even more crowded. "Sorry, Ms. McLean, but we're running behind schedule tonight," the hostess said at the door. "We're hosting a dinner for the local dental society. It'll be at least half an hour before we can get you a table."

Savannah accepted the news graciously and glanced toward the smoky interior of the adjacent bar. "Has Mr. McLean arrived yet?"

"No, ma'am, he hasn't."

"I'll wait in the bar, then. If my grandfather should arrive before the table's ready, please tell him I'm here."

"Will do. And Ms. McLean, the drink is on the house."

"Thanks." Savannah threaded her way past clusters of name-tagged dentists and their wives, finally selecting a stool at the far end of the bar. From her position, she could see the entrance clearly. The bartender hurried over to take her order. She began to relax. She could hear strains of "Tenderly" playing softly in the background. The restaurant was filled with the aroma of freshly baked bread and seafood. Even the hum of voices and muted laughter was vaguely comforting. They made her feel less alone.

The crowd of people jockeying for position at the bar thinned as another group was rounded up and led into the main dining room. She watched them leave, a preoccupied smile on her lips—which faded abruptly when Brendon Sloane stepped into the room.

He said something to the hostess, who gestured and pointed toward the dining room, shaking her head. Then he turned to the bar. He halted when he saw Savannah, a slow smile tugging at his mouth. His eyes widened appreciatively as his roving glance covered her from head to toe.

Recalling the scene at the restaurant earlier that day, Savannah felt embarrassed. But she was determined to face him coolly. He strode lazily toward her, one hand shoved casually in the pocket of his slacks.

"Well, if it isn't the lady who stared at me all during lunch," he teased in a low voice. He wore the same blue suit he'd had on earlier. His blue silk tie was wrapped in a neat Windsor knot and accented with a sterling silver stickpin. "Mind if I sit down?"

Savannah realized she'd been holding her breath. Chiding herself, she replied coolly, "It's a public place." The moment the words were out, she knew she'd sounded too defensive. But he only smiled and leaned closer, one elbow resting against the bar, his powerful chest within inches of her. From the calculating way he was looking down at her, she knew she'd been right to be wary. She recalled Emerson's warning, his unusual and fervent dislike of Brendon Sloane.

"For the record, Ms. McLean, I am *not* trying to pick you up," Brendon informed her with mocking amusement.

Her chin rose at his arrogant tone. "Lose any more hankies lately?" she asked sweetly. "Or are you in the lost-and-found business?"

It was his turn to be chagrined. He sighed, his mouth quirking with telltale guilt. "I had hoped that handkerchief routine would be the means to an introduction. Certainly it got your attention, and in a roundabout way you could say I got my wish." Before she could reply, he'd sat down on the wooden bar stool next to her. The space was narrow, and as his legs brushed hers, static electricity crackled. Savannah's wool skirt clung to his neatly fitting trousers.

"Whoa." Brendon smoothed the errant fabric, detaching her skirt from his pants. His eyes lingered briefly on her exposed thigh, then traveled lazily down to the curve of her calf and the toe of her black sling-back pump. She shivered with awareness.

"Sorry," he apologized. "My hands must be cold from the wind outside."

They were, but that wasn't why she had shivered. What was it about him that reduced her to speechlessness, heightened her senses, and increased her heartbeat? His height? His ease of movement? Was it his intent gaze, the fact that he refused to be put off by her cool reserve?

Brendon faced forward on the stool. Even in the dark bar, she could see the ruddiness in his cheeks. Clasping one fist over the other, he lifted his hands to his mouth and blew lightly, warming his hands with his breath. Savannah was acutely aware of his nearness and of the provocative scent of his cologne.

The bartender returned with her mint julep and turned to Brendon. "What'll it be, Mr. Sloane?"

"Bourbon and branch."

"Coming right up."

"You're very well known," Savannah observed after the bartender had returned with Brendon's drink.

He settled more heavily in his seat. His fingers plucked at the seams of his slacks as he adjusted them more comfortably over his thighs. "I think I've made my mark on this town. Intuition tells me you will too before long."

He smiled at her, and her mouthful of mint julep almost didn't go down. Trying to get a grip on her chaotic emotions and keep a cool head, she sipped the minty liquor through the thin cocktail straw. Seeing his gaze zero in on her mouth, her pulse rate seemed to triple. She licked the moisture from her lips and tried to inject nonchalance into her tone. "Do you come here often?"

"Only when I don't want to be alone," he said softly. Their gazes met, and she was reminded of their staring match earlier, the kiss he had half-teasingly bestowed on the back of her hand. "What about you?" he asked. "What are you doing here tonight?"

"I'm meeting someone," she answered, wishing abruptly that she weren't.

"Anyone I know?" he asked casually before taking another sip of his drink. He stared into the mirror behind the bar. His eyes drifted toward her image.

She glanced toward the entrance. "I'm meeting my grandfather."

Brendon groaned and murmured something unintelligible. "I don't know whether to continue to sit here out of sheer perversity or to run for cover."

She turned toward him, seizing the opportunity to satisfy her curiosity. "What happened between the two of you to make you dislike one another so intensely?"

Brendon shrugged. "Ask Emerson."

"I did. He won't tell me." She held his gaze but was unable to read his expression.

Brendon faced her, one foot hooked over the rung of his stool. "Over the years I've undercut your grandfather on a couple of bids. I don't run my business like a poker game. I prefer to deal in a more straightforward manner. I'm also the new boy on the block, and I've offered your grandfather's firm the first real competition it's felt for almost forty years."

"Where are you from originally?"

"Ohio."

"How long have you been here?"

"Almost five years." Brendon swirled the liquid in his glass with a lazy motion. "What about you? That accent is definitely not South Carolina."

"Oh, I was raised here all right. But I lost most of my drawl when I lived in California. Nothing irritates a Westerner more than that soft Southern drawl. Believe it or not, you can lose a sale because of it."

"I believe it." His eyes trailed the length of her appraisingly and lingered on the soft swell of her breasts beneath her silk blouse before returning to her face. "I also like the sound of your voice."

With effort she ignored his provocative glance. He was making polite conversation, that was all. In a moment he would move on to his table, and she would move to hers. "That's because you've acquired an accent, too." Her tone was cool despite her racing pulse.

"Have I?" He looked surprised.

"It's sort of half-Yankee and half–South Carolina." She propped her chin on her fist and sent him a teasing smile.

She knew she was flirting a little, but she seemed powerless to make herself stop. "You can't live down here long without slipping into some of the gently slurred patterns of speech."

"True."

They fell silent. Brendon's gaze drifted over her again. She was extremely conscious of his physical presence. He had the faint traces of a tan. Tiny grooves were etched in the skin at the corners of his eyes and mouth. Sparse light brown hair feathered the backs of his hands. His palms were calloused, as if he had experienced the rigors of hard physical labor.

"So you were in sales in California," he said. "Real estate, I presume?"

Savannah laughed. "Considering my background, it would have been heresy to go into cars or clothes. I started out selling houses, worked my way into the million-dollar range, got my broker's license, entered management after that, and presided over a sales force of thirteen."

"I'm impressed."

"I learned a lot. Frankly I think anyone considering working in our business ought to progress that way. It lends expertise to one's marketing techniques later on."

Brendon nodded, regarding her with open admiration. "I see why your grandfather was so eager to have you back in Charleston."

She stared down at her hands. It was hard to tell what was making her warmer, the alcohol in her drink or his gaze. His knee pressed lightly against hers, then withdrew. She raised her eyes, and their gazes collided. "Sorry. It's these damn chairs," he said. "My legs never seem to fit."

Glancing down, Savannah saw that he was bunched uncomfortably into a rather small space. She shifted her legs to the side to give him more room.

"Thanks."

A group of people entered the bar, and another group was led off toward the dining room. She breathed a sigh of relief when she saw that Emerson was not among either group.

"Scared to be seen with me?" Brendon taunted softly.

She blushed. "Of course not." But the truth was she didn't want another public scene between the two men.

He stared at her steadily, then took another sip of his drink. "So, how long will you be staying? Are you here permanently, or just until after your grandfather retires and names a new company president?"

"I'm here to stay."

The bartender returned, this time with a phone in his hand. "Ms. McLean," he said, pushing a button, "your grandfather's on line two."

"Thank you." Conscious of Brendon's eyes on her, she lifted the phone to her ear.

Emerson's voice rumbled throatily. "Savannah, I'm sorry, but it looks like I can't make it after all. We've got some problems on this bid, and Frank wants to take me to dinner to discuss them. I offered to take everyone to the Wine Cellar, but he'd already arranged to meet the rest of the school board over at the Barbados Room. I'd ask you to join us, but—"

"Thanks, Grandfather, but I think I'll just sit this one out." She knew Frank's cigar-smoking crowd. Their raucous stories were definitely not for female ears. She glanced over at Brendon, who was still watching her.

"Are you sure you're going to be all right now?" Emerson asked. "I hate standing you up when I promised you dinner."

She laughed. "I'm twenty-eight years old. I think I can make it home alone."

"All right." Emerson sighed. "But be careful. Lock the door after you get in your car. And Savannah, be sure and have some dinner on me before you leave." The phone clicked as he hung up. The bartender removed the phone.

"Emerson's not coming?" Brendon's brow arched speculatively.

"Apparently not." Savannah cupped both hands around her glass and stared straight ahead, feeling unaccountably shy.

"Would you like to have dinner with me?" The pad of

his little finger brushed the back of her knuckles, and a thrill of pure physical pleasure shot through her. "We could share a table. Think of the inconvenience and wait that would save for someone else."

Her heart raced. Her throat was suddenly dry, but she blamed it on the liquor. "I guess we do owe the establishment that much, especially after they plied us with free drinks."

He nodded solemnly. "It's the only thing to do."

She smiled, realizing how much she had missed having dinner with someone her own age. Maybe she and Brendon could be friends. Maybe she could even patch up the bad feelings between Brendon and her grandfather. For the sake of both firms, it was worth a try.

The hostess arrived to tell them the table Emerson had reserved was ready. "I'll be dining with Ms. McLean." Brendon took Savannah's elbow in a light, possessive grasp, and they followed the hostess's trailing aqua gown as she led them to a cozy table.

Brendon pulled out Savannah's chair. The back of his hand pressed lightly against her spine. Instead of taking the seat opposite her, he took the one directly next to her. She was so aware of him, she could barely breathe. Suddenly it seemed as if they had known each other for years. She could imagine him as her lover. She wanted him to be affected by her in the same powerful way she was affected by him.

"Steak, salad, and a baked potato with sour cream," Brendon said, having barely consulted the menu.

"I'll have the same, as well as a bowl of your homemade gumbo."

"Wine?" Brendon asked.

"I have to drive home, so I don't think so."

"Coffee, then?"

"With my ice water, please." The waitress departed. "My first week back I stopped at a restaurant and had not one or two but four servings of their hummingbird cake right in a row." She laughed. "The people thought I was crazy, but

I missed that concoction of pineapple, pecans, bananas, and cream cheese so much while I was away that I couldn't resist."

Brendon studied her. "Is that what brought you back?"

It was an innocent question, but she glanced away, feeling her ebullient mood fade. "I was divorced about a year ago," she said quietly.

"I'm sorry." His tone was kind and not judgmental.

"There didn't seem to be much left for me in California," she continued after the waitress had brought their salads and her soup. "Most of the people we saw socially were also married. It was very difficult to be with them. It was even harder to be single again after all those years of being someone's wife. Here at least I don't have the memories to contend with."

"How long were you married?"

"Five years." Savannah dipped her spoon into the thick, fragrant Southern gumbo, which was brimming with crabmeat, chicken, shrimp, oysters, and a variety of vegetables and spices.

"Do you miss him?"

Brendon's low voice brought her head up. She couldn't tell what he was thinking. She answered honestly, her eyes never leaving his. "Sometimes I miss having someone to come home to at night. I don't miss the fights or the ugliness of a disintegrating relationship."

"I'm sorry," he said softly, dropping his gaze and shaking his head. "I shouldn't have asked that."

"It's okay; it isn't your fault." Impulsively she covered his hand with hers. Touching him warmed her through and through.

She withdrew her hand awkwardly after a moment and continued eating her soup. "What about you?" she asked casually. "What brought you to South Carolina?"

"Survival. The recession closed down a lot of factories in my home state. When the interest rates went up along with inflation, business decreased. I had the choice of relocating and moving my capital to an area where there was industry and people or staying and riding out the economic difficulties in my hometown. I came; I prospered. Five years later I'm still here."

"That must be one of the reasons we've never met," Savannah said. "I would have been in California by the time you arrived."

"I know I would have remembered you." His low voice prompted a smile.

"That goes double, Mr. Sloane."

"Call me Brendon."

"Brendon." She repeated his name, liking the sound of it. She sensed the fast-growing intimacy between them.

During the rest of the meal, they discussed the climate, local saltwater fishing, and historic sites. Brendon insisted on paying for dinner. "It's been my treat," he assured her. His white teeth flashed in a dazzling grin, and warmth suffused her again.

"Well, as delightful as this has been, I really think I had better get home," Savannah finally announced. "I've got a heavy schedule tomorrow, and it's getting late."

"Let me walk you to your car." Brendon rose.

Suddenly she realized she didn't want to be alone with him. She didn't want to face the awkwardness of parting in a dark parking lot. "Really, it's not necessary," she said. "I'll be quite safe."

"No, I wouldn't rest easy knowing you were out there alone."

Not wanting to argue, she let him escort her outside. The night air was cool and filled with the scent of winter-blooming camellias. Brendon's arm steadied her elbow lightly as they picked their way past the rows of cars to Savannah's burgundy Seville. "Thank you for dinner. It really was a lovely evening," she murmured, her back to the door. "Now I owe you a dinner." More than anything, she realized, she wanted to see him again.

"I'd like that. How's your social calendar now that you're back in your hometown? Filled to overbrimming?" he guessed lightly.

She thought of the many invitations she had turned down. "Actually I've been busy at the firm."

"No old beaux beating down your door?"

She shook her head. "Most of my old beaux are married, have moved away, or are what my grandfather would call ineligible."

"I see. I'm glad you're not involved with anyone else." So was she.

The moment drew out awkwardly. She ducked her head. It had been so long since she'd been out on a date or even said a private good night to a man other than her husband. Brendon seemed to sense her nervousness and indecision. "I'll wait while you get out your keys," he said finally.

"All right." Her fingers fumbled through her purse. Finally she located her keys and slid them into the door. The lock clicked open. Disappointment flowed through her as she realized he wasn't going to kiss her.

She opened the door and tossed her purse onto the seat, then turned toward him, planning to say a final polite goodbye. Without a word he glided forward. His hands gripped her shoulders lightly. Her head tilted back, and his mouth came down on hers. With the barest pressure, they fitted lips against lips, moved, shifted to better adjust the alignment of their chins and noses. His kiss deepened slowly, and her mouth opened under his. He invaded her lips with the sweetness of his tongue and she tasted coffee and the spicy sauce that had flavored their steaks. His teeth nudged hers gently; his tongue twined with hers.

She wrapped her arms tighter about his neck and stepped further into the embrace. His arms circled her back, and he held her tightly against him. They stood thigh to thigh, waist to waist, the warmth of his skin flowing into hers. Eventually their breathing slowed and the kiss drew slowly to a halt. She was dizzy and disoriented as she stepped back, her hands trembling slightly. She grasped his forearms and took a deep, steadying breath. Brendon smiled tenderly down at her and let his lips graze her forehead. He clasped her hand and kissed her fingertips lingeringly. "Good night," he murmured softly.

"Good night."

In her rearview mirror she noticed that he waited until

her car was moving out of the parking lot before he turned away. The protective gesture was oddly comforting. She recalled the timbre of his low, masculine voice long after she had arrived home.

CHAPTER
Three

S AVANNAH FACED HER grandfather across his cluttered desk early the next morning. "If you want McLean Development to prosper during the next decade, you're going to have to improve the way you do business immediately."

"Are you referring to the Edisto Island project, by any chance?" Emerson asked.

"It's in trouble," she confirmed.

"What do you mean?" He lit the end of an imported cigar. "I looked at the construction schedule this morning. By crew estimations we're several days ahead of schedule."

"For what you have slated," Savannah agreed. Her eyes met Emerson's unflinchingly. "The problem is, it isn't nearly enough. Your marketing approach is hopelessly out of date. Every other project within sixty miles features its own golf course, tennis courts with resident pro, restaurant, bar, and lounge. All we have planned for the Seascape Villas is a private marina and an Olympic-size swimming pool."

"You have to consider the location, Savannah," Emerson replied calmly. "That project is being built on a strip of magnificent oceanfront property just forty miles south of Charleston. We've raised the town homes one behind the other for spectacular individual views. We've used only the finest materials. We offer one- to four-bedroom plans, with varying amounts of square footage. Those units will sell with or without the additional amenities."

"When have you been content with a mediocre project and usual sales?" she challenged, raising her chin. "You built this firm single-handed, Grandfather. You've stuck with it for nearly half a century, going from a series of low-cost single-family homes to multimillion-dollar apartment complexes, seaside resorts, and ultramodern public buildings. The truth is, as far as the Edisto Island project goes, we can and should do a lot better. If we don't put forth our very best effort, our reputation will suffer."

"Naturally you have a few suggestions to make," Emerson prompted, looking amused.

"I want this project to be a smashing success," she said, "not just another custom-built multifamily complex bearing our firm's name. I don't want it to be simply competitive with what Sloane Construction and other companies are offering. I want it to be ten times better."

"Go on," Emerson urged, leaning back in his chair and propping his feet up on his desk.

"I want to rename the project Paradise, put in an on-site gym, sauna, and whirlpool, exclusive indoor/outdoor bistro, small shopping plaza, and a minisupermarket featuring reasonable prices." She gestured enthusiastically, then paused to hand her grandfather sketches and estimates to study. "I'd like to add hike and bike trails, tennis courts, a golf course, and a restaurant and bar."

"Whoa!" Emerson held up a silencing hand. "Have you looked at the figures you've given me, Savannah? Have you looked at our company books?"

"I met with Harve Webb at the bank this morning. He's agreed to finance the additional construction at below market rates, assuming you and the board of directors approve. We'll also have to raise the sale prices of the condominiums by roughly ten percent, but I think it will be worth the price when you consider the resort atmosphere the Paradise condominiums will have."

Emerson studied the sketches she had handed him. "Savannah, I'm impressed."

"I'd also like to break with tradition and hire an outside firm to help prepare our advertising campaign. We're going to need a very young, fresh approach if we hope to sell the majority of the three-hundred-unit complex by fall."

"Savannah, we'll be lucky to move one hundred of those units by September." Frowning, Emerson reached for his coffee mug.

She took a deep breath, her tension easing. "If we advertised in this area alone, I would agree. But I'm planning to run a multimedia campaign through real estate and investment offices all over the Northeast and mid-Atlantic states. We can't forget Paradise is in a prime vacation area. A lot of our sales will be to young professionals who are interested in owning a home on the shore and commuting to Charleston to work. Many other sales will be to wealthy individuals looking for an oceanfront home. For those who want to use Paradise strictly as a vacation or summer home, we'll offer an on-site security service to guard against break-in or theft. For those who would like to rent or lease their town houses for part of the year, we'll see that that's done, too."

"You're beginning to sound as much of a gambler as Sloane," Emerson complained. "Only his marketing approaches have failed as often as they've succeeded."

Now was the chance to tell Emerson she had had dinner with Brendon last night. She started to speak, then bit her tongue resolutely. She wasn't going to let anything interfere with the work she'd done on the Edisto Island project.

Emerson stacked the sketches neatly in the center of his desk. "I'll present your proposal to the board of directors this afternoon. Assuming they agree—and I feel sure they will—you'll get the budget you want to expand the project."

"I also want total control from this point on—everything from hiring and firing to budget, subcontracting, and sales."

"You've earned it."

"Thank you," Savannah said quietly. She felt the pleasure she always experienced when a sales pitch went well. Because the time and mood seemed right, she added, "Have you given any more thought to who will succeed you when you retire?"

Emerson rose and began pacing the carpeted office, his hands clasped behind his back. For the first time since their meeting began, he did not look directly at her. "Yes, Savannah, I've given it a great deal of thought. I'm sorry. I know how much you want the position, but I'm going to have to give it to John Crawford."

Disappointment surged through her. A sick feeling formed in the pit of her stomach. "Why?" she demanded. "He's made it clear he doesn't want the position. I'm just as qualified."

"You've had a very rough year. It wouldn't hurt for you to have a little more time to settle in." Abruptly Emerson's appeal seemed more personal than professional. He was speaking as her grandfather, not her boss.

"There's more to this decision than a lack of faith in my abilities, isn't there?" she said.

Emerson nodded and sat down. "I'm worried about the long hours you would be forced to put in," he admitted gently. "I lost the affections of my wife and daughter because of the demands this company put on my time. I'm not going to allow you to make the same mistake."

"It wouldn't be a mistake for me." She leaned forward imploringly. "It's what I really want."

Emerson sighed. "I know it seems as if you've got ages left in which to marry and raise a family, but time goes quickly. Before you know it, your chance will have passed you by. And you're too much like me, Savannah. Once you get involved in your work..."

He didn't have to continue. Since returning to Charleston, she had hardly left her office.

"Savannah, I want you to marry, have a satisfying private

life, everything I've missed all these years. The time to devote yourself entirely to the business will come. Your youth and childbearing years won't last forever." He paused and took a deep pull on his cigar. "I don't want you to be in my situation forty years down the road, bemoaning all you've missed. I want a family for you, people you love surrounding you. I know you think I'm being old-fashioned, but I truly do want you to have it all."

Occasionally she did long for a loving husband and children. "It's not that simple," she said wryly. "I can't run out to a soiree featuring eligible men, select the best candidate, take him home, marry him, and start a family." Her voice was light and teasing. She knew Emerson meant well. She'd simply have to cajole him out of his melancholy mood. No doubt his worrisome reflections were brought on by his pending retirement.

"Precisely why you need as much free time as possible," Emerson countered affably. "The more men you date, the better your chances of finding someone compatible. When you do settle down, the company will still be here. In the meantime you'll be awarded a vice-presidency and as much input as you care to offer."

"Aren't you forgetting that I've already tried the state of holy matrimony?" she countered. She'd learned that being married to a man who was less dynamic than she was didn't work. And she had yet to come across anyone who was as devoted and successful in his career and still interested in marriage.

"Try again," Emerson said, dismissing her objection.

They had been through that argument before. Savannah's jaw set with determination. Her grandfather was being ridiculous. How could she make him see that?

Suddenly, as if from nowhere, Brendon Sloane's handsome face came to mind, his dark eyes twinkling mischievously, his sensual mouth quirked wryly, his light hair tousled by the wind. She recalled his long, lean length and sure movements, the touch of his warm hand at the small of her back and his firm lips on her mouth. An idea began to form in her mind.

"Grandfather, suppose I were to marry before you retired. What then? Would I still have a chance at presiding over the firm April first?"

He shrugged. "This is all castles in the air, Savannah."

"Humor me, then, and answer my question. What would happen if I were to marry before you retired?"

He frowned and stubbed out his cigar. "Yes, I suppose I would award you the presidency. But frankly, Savannah, given your attitude about marriage and men, I don't foresee that happening."

A small smile lifted the corners of her mouth. "We'll see, Grandfather. We'll see."

Savannah didn't know whether to be exasperated or amused. Emerson needed to have his consciousness raised and be shown that she could run McLean Development and have a satisfying personal life as well. Talking to him hadn't helped. If she insisted on pursuing the issue verbally, she knew he would become annoyed with her nagging.

What she needed was a vivid, dramatic way to make her grandfather realize exactly what he was asking of her. He needed to see her with a totally unsuitable man. If she pretended to be serious about her new beau, Emerson would no doubt change his mind about her marrying. With that issue out of the way, maybe she could persuade him to award her the presidency of the family firm. She had done everything possible to earn the position.

On a more practical level, she needed to ease the tension between Brendon and her grandfather and find a way to tell Emerson she'd had dinner with his rival. She wanted to see Brendon again, but only with Emerson's knowledge and approval.

It was a complex tangle of problems, and she spent the rest of the morning thinking about them. By noon she felt she had a clear view of the dilemma and, even more important, a swift and dramatic way of solving it. After all, actions always spoke louder than words, and Emerson did enjoy a good practical joke. The question was, would Brendon agree to help? Did she dare ask him? She had to figure out how to phrase such a request without offending him. Would he understand the importance of her goals—a private life subject to no interference, and a truce between the owners of two powerful competing firms?

Deciding that there was no time like the present to find out, she informed her secretary that she was leaving the office and would be gone the rest of the day.

It was harder than she'd imagined to track down Brendon. She discovered that he was rarely in his Calhoun Street office, because he liked to be wherever his firm was building. He did lunch often in the many hotels around town. But by the time she reached the Chapel Market Place restaurant, where his secretary had indicated he would dine that day, he had already left. So much for the casual, unplanned approach.

Savannah made a three o'clock appointment with Brendon and arrived at his office precisely two minutes before the hour. He was still in conference. At the secretary's direction, she took a seat in the waiting room. She was wearing a vibrant red silk high-collared blouse, a black velvet blazer, and a red-and-black tartan plaid wool skirt. Dark stockings and calf-hugging black suede boots completed her winter ensemble. Outwardly she was prepared. Inwardly she was a bundle of nerves. Her hands were damp with perspiration and her stomach was dancing with butterflies.

Maybe this was a bad idea. Maybe, despite her willingness to act as liaison, the two construction firms would never be able to do business together. Maybe in reality Brendon Sloane had no sense of humor. Just because *she'd* enjoyed their dinner together didn't mean the evening had carried any special significance for him. His kiss had been very experienced, but just because it had wreaked havoc on her senses didn't mean—

Without warning the door to his office opened and Brendon Sloane stood on the threshold. "Sorry to keep you waiting." He smiled. "I was on the phone, long distance. Won't you come in?"

He seemed taller than she remembered, the width of his

shoulders more intimidating. His blue-gray pinstripe suit
moulded to his lean body. Confidence radiated from him as
she strode into the room.

His office was as sleek and modern as the waiting room.
The walls were papered in a silvery damask; the carpet was
a light oyster hue. In front of a low white sofa covered in
a nubby-textured cotton fabric, stood a glass-topped coffee
table. Noting the austere bookcases, a large teakwood desk,
and a comfortable swivel chair, Savannah sat in one of the
twin slingback chairs facing the windows. Brendon perched
on the edge of his desk. "How's your day been?" he asked.

Had it been just the night before that he'd kissed her? It
seemed eons ago. Could he sense how attracted she was to
him? Did he feel the same?

"I've been busy," she answered, relieved to hear that her
voice sounded composed.

"Me, too." His gaze dropped to her crossed leg, and she
fought the urge to pull her skirt further down over her knee.

Brendon leaned forward slightly, and Savannah felt her
breath catch in her chest. His teeth bit his lower lip, then
parted slightly. His gaze narrowed disarmingly. "So tell me,
Savannah," he said softly, "why have you been chasing me
all over town?"

CHAPTER
Four

MOMENTARILY HER COURAGE deserted her. Her scheme to resolve all her problems suddenly seemed silly. Brendon was still waiting for an explanation. "I'd like to invite you to dinner," she said finally, her voice husky with tension. She blamed it on her lack of experience and the fact that she'd never before pursued a man. Knowing it was too late to back out, she flashed him an artificially bright smile and clarified, "Tonight, if you're free."

Brendon's eyes widened with interest. Once more his gaze drifted lazily down before returning to her face. There was a significant pause as he studied her silently. "And where should this dinner take place?" he inquired in a low, intimate tone that sent shivers down her spine. "Am I to be treated to a home-cooked meal at your apartment?"

Heat flared in her cheeks. He thought she was coming on to him! "Actually I had something more formal in mind." She kept her tone calculatedly cool.

"Oh?" His brows rose.

"I live in the carriage house on my grandfather's estate," she explained, folding her hands together primly. She hesitated, wondering why she was being so guarded. The tip of her tongue wet her lower lip.

His lambent gaze focused on the movement. "The carriage house doesn't have a kitchen?" he inquired smoothly.

"It has a wonderful kitchen." She cleared her throat and took a steadying breath. It took every bit of determination not to react to the delicious feelings of longing his sensual regard evoked. As attracted as she was to him, she knew she had to keep her goals in mind. If and when peace was made between Brendon and her grandfather, then she could pursue a friendship with Brendon. Until then it was senseless to play with fire, and Brendon was definitely a very virile flame. "I just thought it would be easier if we ate in the main house."

"With Emerson," Brendon ascertained carefully.

"Yes." He didn't seem as surprised by the invitation as she'd expected him to be. She fought her feeling of unease, attributing it to her nervousness in the unaccustomed role of pursuer. "His housekeeper, Tammy Jo, is a marvelous cook, and frankly I can't do much with either spatula or spoon."

He grinned as if at a private joke. Rising restlessly, he rounded his desk and settled in the contoured chair, his elbows on the armrests, his hands pressed together in front of him. "You haven't told your grandfather we had dinner together last night, have you?"

She swallowed. Now they were getting down to the difficult part. She only hoped she could explain her plan to Brendon's satisfaction. "In good conscience, I can't see you again on the sly," she said.

Brendon remained motionless. When he exhaled he seemed to relax slightly. "I wouldn't think you'd need me present to tell Emerson we met by accident at the Wine Cellar and after a drink agreed to have dinner together." He was watching her tirelessly. Savannah hadn't a clue to what was going on in his head. Had she overestimated his ability to enjoy a joke? Would he even understand why she wanted to play it?

"I don't need you there to tell him." She glanced awkwardly past him, toward the gray winter landscape.

"Then why do you want me to come to dinner?" he asked quietly.

His steady gaze made her pulse race. She was glad she was sitting down; she didn't think her legs would support her. "I did promise to treat you to a meal," she said lamely.

"And that's all?" His gaze forced her blue eyes down.

"Actually it's a little more complicated than that." She too rose to roam restlessly to the window. Even in the dead of January, Charleston, South Carolina, was a lovely city, spectacular with its beautifully preserved antebellum homes, historic shrines, and wonderfully maintained churches. Lovely gardens interspersed with live oaks and palmettos decorated the winding city streets. For some reason the sight calmed her and made her feel close to the man she had come to bargain with. Some instinct told her she could trust him. Impulsively she decided to tell him everything.

"Emerson won't let me become president of McLean Construction. He's convinced that the key to my fulfillment is through marriage, the traditional roles of wife and mother. I admit I sometimes long for someone to share my life with," she said softly, forgetting for a moment just where she was. Brendon's chair creaked behind her as he rose. "But I'm not going to marry just anyone to please my grandfather. Neither will I sacrifice my work. It's all I've got left, the force that's sustained me during the turmoil of the past year. It's my future. It's my passion."

"Why would you have to give up your work?" Brendon came to her side and leaned against the window frame. His breath was so close, it stirred her hair and made smoky circles on the glass. The provocative, musky scent of his aftershave engulfed her, deepening the feeling of intimacy between them. Her thoughts returned to the night before and his kiss. Was he remembering, too?

She stared up into his rugged face. Seeing a small place where he'd nicked himself shaving, she wanted to lift her finger and smooth the hurt away. Realizing that she had an instinctive desire to comfort him disturbed her almost as much as his nearness. "Would you want a wife who worked?" she asked.

His glance lowered and he crossed his arms. "I wouldn't want a wife who didn't."

She grinned wryly, feeling a familiar bitterness close around her. "That's a very commendable, liberated view." She sighed. "Unfortunately, my previous husband didn't share it."

"He wanted you to quit?" Brendon asked softly, his brows coming together in a frown.

"No." Her voice was low and tinged with irony as she stared out the window. "We needed the income from my salary. But when I was offered a vice-presidency at the firm where I worked, he asked me to turn it down." She sighed again, remembering her pain. "Keith felt the hours would jeopardize our relationship."

"I see," Brendon said gently. "And did you turn it down?" He touched her shoulder lightly. She glanced up.

"Yes." She swallowed, fighting a feeling of hopelessness. "Later, when our relationship fell apart anyway and we did divorce, another opening came up. I was passed over. My superiors were sorry, but they couldn't be sure I wouldn't marry again and abandon or cut back on my professional responsibilities. It was at about that time my grandfather announced his plans to retire and asked me to come home. I knew I didn't have a future in California. I felt I had a chance for a fresh start here. But now I'm up against the same sort of discrimination. Unless I can get my grandfather to change his mind, all my hard work will have been for nothing."

"I'm sorry," Brendon said softly.

She shrugged. "It's a valuable lesson. At the moment I'm concerned about my future. I want to live up to my potential. I can't do that unless Emerson awards me the presidency."

The silence lengthened between them. She was intensely aware of everything about Brendon. Daylight streamed into the office, highlighting his hair. She itched to discover whether it was coarse or soft to the touch. Longing swept over her. She wanted to be held and kissed by him again. But she yearned for more than his touch and caresses. She wanted to be understood. Brendon seemed capable of both. But appearances could be deceiving, Savannah reminded herself firmly. And she didn't know him well enough yet even to begin entertaining such frankly desirous thoughts.

As she turned away a silky black strand of hair fell across her cheek. Brendon gently brushed it behind her ear. His touch was warm and compelling, his gaze understanding. Savannah was melting all over again, no longer sure she wanted to resist the powerful emotions that drew her to him.

"I don't understand what all this has to do with dinner or me," he said at length.

"I'm coming to that." She straightened and walked back to the desk, knowing that the only way she could keep her thoughts from straying was to maintain a physical distance between them. "It's no secret that I'm going to inherit McLean Development eventually. My mother lives in Europe and has no interest in the firm. My grandmother's dead, so aside from me there's no one to take it over. John Crawford could step in for a while, but because of his chronic ulcer, it would only be a temporary solution. Emerson has promised me the presidency someday. We both know I'm qualified and could handle the job now. But he insists that I get married first. He thinks the presidency is too demanding to allow me the time I'll need to find someone else and get back into circulation socially. Don't misunderstand. Most of the time Emerson is a perfectly reasonable man, and I love him dearly. But in this case he's way off the mark. Naturally I've tried talking to him, but it just hasn't worked. So I began thinking along more dramatic lines. Emerson's always enjoyed a joke."

"For that matter, so do all the rest of the men in this community." Brendon grimaced.

A tingle of unease crept down Savannah's spine. "You don't approve of them?"

"On the contrary, I've never been invited to join in."

His face was so unreadable it was infuriating. Didn't he have a sense of humor? "What was your idea?" His words were clipped.

Despite his lack of humor, he still seemed to want to help. She continued more carefully. "I thought I'd take a man home, someone my grandfather would find less than admirable."

His smile flashed, but masculine resentment flared in his dark eyes. "And after the ruckus at the Mills House Hotel, you naturally thought of me," he guessed.

Savannah cringed, suddenly realizing how insensitive her words must have sounded. "I'm sorry. That didn't come out right. I'm nervous. When I am, I tend to run my words together." She raised her hand in helpless agitation. Her heart was pounding, her mouth dry. "If I've offended you—"

"For the record, I think you've worded your intentions quite accurately." Brendon pushed away from the window and strode lazily to her side.

Was he being sarcastic? She couldn't tell. Knowing she couldn't leave with a misunderstanding between them, she tried again. "Emerson must be made to understand that my private life is my own. Whether or not I ever date and remarry is my decision. I won't let him push me into anything before I'm ready. Neither will I let him refuse me the presidency for such a chauvinistic reason. I gave up one promotion on a male demand. I won't lose a second if I can help it. It's Emerson's decision. According to the by-laws of our corporation, he can appoint whomever he wants to succeed him. So I have to change his mind."

"And you want me to help." His tone was chilling.

Savannah studied his impassive expression. She *had* offended him. Damn! "I thought maybe after the joke we'd all be friends. I guess I—miscalculated. I—these pranks are sort of a tradition. But how would you know that unless you have been raised here and participated in some of them?" Her voice ran down like a motor out of fuel. "At one time or another nearly everyone in the community has participated in at least one joke."

A corner of Brendon's mouth lifted in an enigmatic smile. "Good point. Maybe it's high time I got more involved." He shifted closer until they stood only inches apart. She was conscious of the flexed muscles of his thighs, the snug fit of material across his lean hips. His suit jacket hung open, revealing his trim waist. She resisted the urge to reach out and discover if his abdomen was really as taut as it looked.

"I can see what's in this for you," Brendon continued quietly at length, "but what happens if this scheme of yours doesn't achieve the desired results? You saw the way Emerson reacted to me the other day. Who's to say a prank like this wouldn't increase his anger?"

"I hadn't thought of that." Savannah worried her lower lip. "I guess there's a risk involved, though to be blunt, I think it's a small one or I wouldn't be here. My grandfather has always been a very good sport. He admires the ability to stand back and look honestly at oneself as well as at others. He feels that a sense of humor is a sign of good character."

"I see. I can't argue with that." Brendon strolled back to his desk, picked up a paperweight, and shifted it from hand to hand. "Next question, then. Are you willing to make it worth my while?" His chin had a roguish tilt, and his eyes sparkled.

Savannah shot him a humorously aggravated glance. "Since I'm taking up your valuable time, I suppose I could repay the favor in a business sense, as in a kindness from my construction firm to yours. The terms would have to be mutually agreeable and equitable."

His teeth flashed in a rakish grin. He dropped the paperweight back onto the corner of his desk and returned to her side. "A businesswoman through and through, aren't you?"

"When I see something I want, I go after it," she said simply. At least in her professional life, she amended silently.

"What happens if I ask for a more personal form of

payment, Savannah?" he teased with husky innuendo. "Then what?"

Warmth flooded her cheeks, and her mouth twisted in a wry grin. Darn him for destroying her composure! "Then I guess I'd have to turn you down."

He sighed expressively, his eyes glinting with an enigmatic light. "Ah, hell, why not? I've never been averse to well-intentioned ribbing, and in this case I owe Emerson McLean. As long as we're going to be partners in crime, though, I'd like to add a few suggestions of my own." He came closer, one hand raised. "You're right. Bringing me home would be a shock. But after all, it is just one date, and an ill-advised one at that."

"You're saying this scam won't work." No matter how hard she tried to concentrate on what he was suggesting, her gaze drifted back to his hands, his chest, his soft and pliant mouth. She kept remembering his kiss. She imagined the way those same lips would feel making a lazy trail over her bare skin, and a thrill shot through her.

"As you outlined it, I'd say your plan has less than a ten percent chance of success. However, if Emerson had the impression that we were seriously involved, the results would be much different."

Savannah sank into a chair. "How seriously involved?" she asked warmly at the same time that the suggestion made a secret thrill turn her knees weak.

"We could pretend to be madly in love."

She laughed nervously. He must have read her mind! She struggled to appear calm. "My grandfather would never believe that," she asserted coolly.

"He'd be shocked, but I think we could convince him." Brendon smiled lazily, and his eyes danced with devilish confidence. "That is, if you're truly committed to the endeavor and want the presidency as much as you say you do."

"I want it," she confirmed with soft defiance. His skepticism made her angry. "How do you suggest we get our point across?" she asked levelly.

Brendon waved his hand. "Passionate glances, whispered endearments, the soft touch of my hands on your shoulder. Come on, Savannah, use your imagination. If you want to end the marriage nonsense with Emerson once and for all, you're going to have to come on strong when you see him this afternoon, make him think you're serious about 'the worst scoundrel in the state.' If that doesn't change his mind about rushing you into another marriage, I don't know what will."

"That's wicked," she accused, warming to his roguish grin. She ached to answer his smile but didn't dare. He was too confident as it was.

"It will work," he emphasized calmly.

Yes, it probably would. "All right, but we can't drag it on too long," she cautioned. "I don't want Emerson need-lessly upset."

She leaned forward in her chair. As Brendon offered a hand to assist her to her feet, his fingers lingered a fraction longer than necessary, sliding around to encircle and caress the underside of her wrist. Savannah's breath suspended in her chest as she felt the tingling of sexual attraction all the way down to her toes. "Beginning a little early, aren't you?" she said, mentally cursing the tremor in her voice.

"You didn't seem to mind the other night," he reminded her, bringing her slowly to his side. One hand slid beneath her silk-lined blazer and moved around her hips to the small of her back. He pressed her intimately against him.

"But this is the office." She fought the flutter of heat in her middle, the automatic tautness of her breasts. She could feel her nipples pressing against the thin lace of her bra and wondered if he could see them imprinted on the equally thin red silk of her blouse.

Brendon lifted her wrist to his mouth and pressed light kisses from back to front. "We need practice if we're going to make this devoted-lovers routine look convincing," he murmured. The edge of his tongue slipped beneath the cuff of her blouse, sending another riotous shiver up her spine. Savannah ordered herself to break the embrace at once, but her feet and arms refused to move. She despised herself for the weakness but seemed equally powerless to do anything about it. "Don't worry," Brendon said, letting go of her wrist. He straightened and peered down at her, loosened the knot of his tie, and casually released the first button on his shirt. "No one is going to disturb us."

The breath stole from her lungs. Her heart pounded so loudly, she thought she could hear it. His head drew closer. His inviting mouth hovered above her own. She felt the last of her control slipping away. Reminding herself firmly where they were, she wedged both hands against the solid wall of his chest. "Brendon, we're due at my grandfather's right now—or at least I am. I didn't mention I was bringing anyone with me."

"So much the better," he murmured, focusing his attention on her mouth. She turned her head swiftly to the side, evading him, and his lips slid delicately across her jawline, sending another sweet rush of longing into the fiery ache in her middle.

"Brendon . . ." Her protest sounded like a soft, low moan.

"I'm just being practical." He sighed, kissing his way around to the other side of her chin. He lifted her hair and his mouth burrowed into the perfumed arch of her neck. His tongue found the sensitive spot behind her ear, and another shudder suffused her frame. "Think how much more convincing our joke is going to be when you arrive slightly late, your hair all mussed, your lips soft and tender from kissing." He straightened and, still holding her close, studied her face. "Even now you've got two spots of color in your cheeks. Ten to one"—he paused, pressing another light kiss over her mutely protesting mouth—"that blush will still be there when we arrive."

It certainly would if he had anything to do with it. Savannah pushed him determinedly away. But she didn't get far, as his hands were still firmly locked around her back, one splaying intimately low. She could feel the rising heat of his desire molding against her. "We don't have to make it this good!" she retorted firmly.

Brendon smiled wryly. "There's one thing you should know about me, Savannah. I never do anything halfway.

When we walk in that door to your grandfather's mansion, he's going to know you've met your match."

Her mouth opened, but her quick reply was smothered by the swift, determined brush of his lips. His tongue slid into her mouth, taking, exploring, wandering at will. He kissed her as if he meant to possess her. Her first impulse was to surrender to the driving dominance of his embrace and enjoy the pleasure he offered. But this was nothing more than a game to him. She tore her mouth from his. "Stop!" she demanded breathlessly, unbidden heat creeping into her cheeks.

"Why?"

"Because I can't think—or breathe—when you kiss me like that." Her fists pressed against his chest. What she'd intended as a defensive gesture ended as a tantalizing caress.

"Do you need to think?" he murmured.

"If I'm to keep a grip on reality, yes. This is a place of business, for heaven's sake!"

"It's also my private office." His eyes strayed to her mouth. He smiled lazily, infuriatingly, then let his gaze drift back up to her own angry eyes. "Where's your sense of adventure?"

Still holding her firmly with one hand, he brought the tip of his index finger to her lips and caressed the lower curve. She wanted to shake her head free but couldn't, held motionless by her own desire. Her breath rose and fell rapidly. His eyes traced the agitated movement. "You seemed so full of mischief a few moments ago," he noted, dropping his hand. His mouth moved warmly across the top of her hair as his fingers slid beneath her jacket to trace her spine. Her effort to avoid his exploring hand only caused her breasts to arch more fully against his chest.

"That was before you started this practice session," she muttered. His tongue was like fire, temptingly caressing the outer lobe of her ear. She turned her head away from him again, but the movement only gave him better access to the slope of her perfumed neck. She moaned at his exquisite touch.

"That perfume you're wearing is incredible," Brendon

confided. "I remember it from the other night. Or is it just the scent of your skin?" His lips made teasing forays from the edge of her collar to her ear. Another riptide of response shot through her.

"Brendon, please," she pleaded very softly. "Stop it." The knowledge that he was teasing her only slightly lessened her physical response.

"One kiss, Savannah, and then I'll let you go."

His cool demand sent her head back up. She read the challenge in his gaze. "What happens if I say no?"

He smiled, once more the rogue, and issued an exaggerated sigh. "Frankly, Savannah, I could do this all day."

She didn't know whether to kick him in the shin or comply, though she knew which activity promised more pleasure. She also knew which would win her freedom first, without attracting the attention of a curious and probably gossipy office staff. She frowned, hating the thought of capitulating to his goading. "All right," she conceded finally. "I'll kiss you once." She ignored the silent voice that said she had wanted that all along. "But you should know I'm only doing this in the interest of our mutual endeavor."

"I can see what a supreme sacrifice you'll be making." His lips curved in maddening irony.

"I'm not a Southern belle who'll swoon at the mere suggestion of an ill-advised kiss," she informed him with exasperation.

He molded her to him so that from knee to waist they were perfectly aligned and touching lightly. "Oh, I know exactly why you're doing this, Savannah," he taunted softly. He increased his grip with a tender-rough movement designed, no doubt, to excite her. "Now let's see how good you are at feigning passion. Because if you can't or won't kiss me like you mean it, we haven't got a prayer in heaven of making this prank work. And I never enter a losing proposition."

Although his arms were surrounding her, he didn't help her. She had to stand on tiptoe to reach his mouth, curl her fingers in the shimmering lightness of his hair, and gently press the back of his head down to touch her mouth to his.

He stood unresponsively, almost indifferently, as she outlined his lips gently with her own. Resentment engulfed her, followed swiftly by the need to show up his pretense of disinterest as surely as he had exposed her own. She lifted her mouth closer, higher, deepened the kiss with her own lightly probing tongue. She invaded his mouth, testing, provoking. When he stiffened and drew slightly back, she ran her tongue impishly over the edges of his teeth, nipped at his lips with her own, then toured his mouth with voluptuous leisure.

"Savannah," he said, his arms closing securely around her. And then he was capitulating completely, groaning and pulling her against him, his hand sliding from her hips to her waist to her shoulders. His mouth ravaged hers, then worshiped it tenderly. He took, possessed, and commanded, orchestrating her surrender and then deliberately seducing her into even further abandon. Her breath caught in her throat, and a delicious yearning swept through her.

Brendon wove his fingers through her tangled hair. When she felt her lungs would burst from the lack of air, he slowly broke off the caress. His lips wandered across her jaw to her ear and buried themselves in the curve of her neck for long, tumultuous seconds. Her pulse speeded crazily. She had deliberately provoked him into responding, but she hadn't planned this white-hot current of desire.

At last Brendon drew back and stared down at her for long moments. A sigh rippled along his lean length. "I think Emerson McLean's got a damn sight more to worry about than even *I* know," he said. "You're one hell of a woman, Savannah McLean."

CHAPTER
Five

THEY DROVE THEIR respective cars to Emerson's mansion. Savannah took the lead in her burgundy Seville, and Brendon followed in a sleek white Mercedes SL coupe. She was glad for the time alone. His advances had caught her by surprise.

No doubt he really was preparing for the outrageous prank they planned to play on her grandfather. Brendon had been a perfect gentleman the night they'd had dinner at the Wine Cellar. She smiled to herself, adding silently, Brendon, you may not know it, but you're being formally presented to one of the scions of Charleston society this afternoon in the most rakish way possible. She couldn't help but hope that his part in the ruse would firmly entrench him in the hell-raising but respected good-old-boy network of which Emerson was a part.

Brendon parked behind Savannah on the historic tree-

lined cobblestone street. Together they approached the wis-
teria-covered red brick courtyard behind black wrought iron
gates. She glanced up at the imposing four-story mansion
and the towering cover of moss-draped live oaks. From the
windows on the uppermost floor, one could see the boat-
filled harbor and Cooper River. She'd spent hours there as
a child, watching the ships and tugboats.

Brendon gallantly took her arm. "Nervous?" he asked
softly.

She thought of all that was at stake. "Yes."

"Well, don't ruin it now by panicking," he advised confidently. "Your instincts are good. Think of it like a poker
game. We've got the winning hand. All you have to do is
stay in the game and bluff your way through." If only she
had his steely nerves.

Emerson's housekeeper answered the door. "Tammy Jo,
I'd like you to meet Brendon Sloane," Savannah murmured
as they stepped inside.

"Your grandfather's in the drawing room. Shall I tell
him you're here?" the red-haired housekeeper asked, fa-
voring Brendon with a wide smile.

"Actually I think Savannah would like to surprise him,"
Brendon demurred. Together they walked across the Ori-
ental carpet that covered the parquet floor of the spacious
front hall. The double doors of the drawing room were
standing open. Rich scarlet damask and silk brocade covered
the windows. Matching fabric adorned both the walls and
oval-backed Louis XVI chairs. Nineteenth-century James
Pollard hunt scenes decorated the walls. An ornate Louis
XVI gold leaf mirror hung next to the imposing portal.
Savannah could see Emerson standing with his back to them.
Drink in hand, he appeared immersed in a complicated business phone call.

"As you can see, we've used wallpapers of fabrics from
historical Charleston," Savannah said nervously as they
waited in the hall. She was deeply conscious of the strength
in Brendon's warm grip, of the fluid movement of his thighs.
She swallowed hard. "Many of the antiques in the drawing
or sitting room are authentic, although an equal number of

them are simply expert reproductions of eighteenth-century
styles."

"Lovely," Brendon murmured appreciatively. He lifted
her hand and bestowed a soft, lingering kiss on first the
underside and then the back of her hand. His eyes held hers
boldly. "Imagine," he whispered with a disbelieving shake
of his head. "A week ago, knowing the way your grandfather
felt about me, you couldn't have paid me to enter this mansion. Now . . ."

His lips moved to her wrist and pressed moistly against
her rapid pulse. Her hands curled into the lapel of his wool
blazer as she swayed unsteadily against him. What was it
about this man that drew her to him so inexorably?

In the drawing room Emerson hung up the phone. As he
turned toward them, his jaw dropped open. A seemingly
interminable pause ensued, fraught with tension. Once he
recovered—and Savannah noted it took him a second—
Emerson straightened, took a deep breath, and moved forward courteously. "Well, Savannah, I wondered where you
were."

"I've invited Brendon to dinner, Grandfather. I thought
it was time for you to get to know my new beau."

The fireworks she had been expecting didn't come, though
the tension was palpable. Emerson didn't swear, stomp his
foot, or glare. She attributed his reaction to good breeding
and a strong sense of Southern hospitality, and prepared
herself for a long and tedious evening.

But Brendon obviously favored a more direct approach.
He shook his head and gave a dramatically long sigh. "Why
you Southerners insist on false cordiality I'll never know."

"It's called manners, son," Emerson said stiffly.

Brendon's lip curled. "Go ahead. Throw caution to the
winds," he dared the older man. "Treat us to your real
thoughts and tell us quite bluntly how you feel about your
granddaughter's new beau."

"I'd be glad to," Emerson replied, setting his drink aside,
"but there's a lady in the room."

"Hold it." Savannah took a deep breath and stepped
between the two men, her hands extended like a traffic cop

in the middle of a dangerous intersection. The last thing they needed was an out-and-out brawl.

"Savannah, why did you bring this reprobate into my home?" Emerson demanded.

Brendon started past her, his hands placed defiantly on his hips. "So now we're name-calling, hm?"

She grabbed Brendon's arm, halting him mid-stride. "Don't you think you're overreacting? In case you didn't notice, my grandfather was trying to be polite." They didn't need to make that much of an impact on Emerson, she decided.

Brendon was instantly contrite. "I'm sorry. You're right. We shouldn't be quarreling, especially when we have such exciting news to relate."

Emerson cast her a wary glance. "I can explain all this," she said, though she quavered at the reproach in his gaze. Perhaps it was time to call off the charade.

"Fortunately, *you* don't have to." Brendon stepped forward and clamped his hands on her shoulders. His steely grip threw her thoughts into disarray. "Savannah knew she couldn't do it alone," he continued smoothly. "And frankly I agree. Sir, Savannah and I have come to confess our involvement."

Savannah's knees sagged. She hadn't expected him to be quite so blunt. Brendon hooked a tenacious arm around her waist and turned her to face him. "It's all right, sweetheart," he said soothingly before she could voice an objection. "Emerson will understand when we tell him we're in love."

Brendon's words were very deliberate. His eyes stared willfully into hers. She recalled what he had said earlier about staying in the game and bluffing their way through. Was that what he was trying to do? Couldn't he see that that wasn't necessary? She'd already succeeded in shocking her grandfather. Surely he'd give her the presidency now.

"Savannah, is this some kind of joke because I've expressed my desire to see you married?" Emerson demanded sternly.

"It's no joke, sir," Brendon countered evenly. "I knew

from the moment I met her that Savannah was a very special woman." He glanced at her lovingly, then turned back to her grandfather, adding, "Which is why I've decided to make her my wife."

Wife! The word echoed in Savannah's mind. Brendon was overplaying his hand to what very well might be a disastrous end. Her grandfather looked just as stunned as she felt. She tried to formulate an explanation that would calm Emerson and prevent Brendon from taking the ruse any further, but nothing coherent came to mind.

She gave Brendon a stern look. "Darling—"

"I know, sweetheart. It's a shock to Emerson, but we've got to lay all our cards on the table. Now is as good a time as any." His intense expression held her spellbound. What was he planning?

"Savannah, is this true?" Emerson demanded in disbelief.

She swallowed, not knowing whether to confess or run for cover and let Brendon explain the truth. She extricated herself from his hold. "Believe me, grandfather, I had no idea it would go so far so quickly." She took a deep, steadying breath. "However, now that it has—"

"We'd like your approval," Brendon cut in easily. He smiled, moving debilitatingly between the two McLeans.

Emerson strolled to the bar and poured a generous dash of whiskey into a glass. He glanced contemplatively from one to the other. Savannah hadn't a clue to what he was thinking. "Of course, if the two of you have been seeing one another..." he mused thoughtfully.

"Naturally we wanted to tell you of our attraction for one another." Still playacting with amazing ease, Brendon circled behind Savannah, wrapped both arms about her waist, and drew her resolutely against him. His steel-under-silk grip was too powerful to be bucked. She felt trapped. Emerson, meanwhile, seemed to be plotting his own coup d'etat.

"Relax and follow my lead," Brendon whispered encouragingly in her ear. "I know what I'm doing. Trust me." The tender skin at her temples was chafed slightly by the five o'clock shadow on his square chin. She was engulfed by the pleasant aroma of his aftershave. Maybe once the joke was over she could convince Emerson to halt the cold war between the two men.

"You haven't been very receptive to Brendon, Grandfather," Savannah pointed out calmly, recalling the scene he'd caused at the Mills House Hotel.

"I guess I haven't been, have I?" Emerson stared contemplatively into his drink.

"The open hostility between you isn't good for the public relations of either firm," she continued.

Emerson glanced worriedly at them, then zeroed in on her. "I know I asked you to begin dating again—"

"I have. At least I've been out with Brendon," she amended. "Informally."

"What she means is we haven't gone public except once or twice," Brendon cut in. "That day in the Mills House Hotel, for instance—" He grinned as if he was taking credit for much more than a simple dinner together.

Emerson paled and glanced back at Savannah for confirmation. "You really *are* involved with this man, aren't you?"

"Up to my neck, it seems." She smiled tightly. Brendon's hands were running sensually up and down her arms. Tingles sparked wherever he touched. Angry with him for seizing control of her scam, she broke free of his grasp. Brendon arched his brows in response but made no attempt to stop her. She relaxed.

Emerson cleared his throat. "In any case, I think it's too soon for you to be married."

Savannah immediately recognized her chance to make her grandfather see how irrational he was being about the company presidency.

"I suppose you've got a point," she said. "It's only been a year since my divorce. Then again, what better time than the present . . . and my childbearing days are about over . . ."

Emerson scowled. "Now, Savannah, you don't need to be in so much of a rush."

"Oh, no?" she said calmly. "That's not what you said the other day."

"Then I was wrong," Emerson said with exasperation.

"Perhaps about handing over the company presidency, too?" she suggested.

Immediately her grandfather's expression changed. He walked back to the windows and stared out. She knew at once that things weren't going the way she'd planned. Damn! She didn't know what to do. Brendon seemed equally puzzled. "All right, sweetheart, I know when I'm licked," Emerson said finally, turning back to them both with a confident, challenging grin. "Of course you can marry Brendon if you want to. When will we set the date?"

For a nightmarish moment she saw herself slipping into the black abyss of a practical joke that had gone totally berserk. There would be no company presidency, no marriage, no Brendon, no friendship between the two firms. She'd gotten them all into a terrible mess. And she didn't know if she would ever be able to explain her way out without making matters even worse.

Brendon seemed to sense her dismay. "How about a celebrative toast?" he suggested, propelling her into a brocade chair. Once she was seated, he strode to the bar. The two men exchanged a long, tension-filled glance. She had no idea what either of them was thinking, but at least they weren't arguing openly.

"You've surprised us, Emerson," Brendon admitted, pouring each of them a shot of bourbon doused liberally with soda. "Savannah and I didn't expect congratulations to come quite so quickly."

"Now that I've accepted the liaison, we might as well formalize the plans." Emerson sent her a level look.

She managed a weak smile. "I don't think I'm ready to set the date," she said quietly, leaning back in her chair. If Emerson thought she would cry uncle; he had another guess coming, particularly when he was looking so smug!

"Personally I've always thought Savannah would make a lovely spring bride," Emerson declared. He turned to her with an overly bright smile. "I know you've been married before, darling, but I still think a white dress would be nice."

That did it. Savannah sat up ramrod straight ready to

reveal the whole embarrassing truth. But before she could speak, Brendon handed her a drink, dropped down on a bent knee, planted a tender kiss near her ear, and said with utter seriousness, "Confess now and I will personally see that you never succeed in business here." The iron will in his low tone made her freeze. What in heaven's name had gotten into him?

Emerson was watching them both carefully. Savannah turned back to Brendon. "You can't mean that," she whispered back.

He smiled, but his jaw was rigid with resolve. "I do." She swallowed. What was going on? What had she gotten herself into?

"Something wrong, darling?" Emerson asked.

"Nothing I can't handle," she answered. Did Brendon have something else up his sleeve? Another wild card? Was that why he insisted they play the charade to the bitter end?

She turned back to Emerson, hoping to salvage whatever was left of her composure. "Frankly, Grandfather, it's not the details of the wedding that concern me. It's the presidency of McLean Development and who will be recommended to replace you upon your retirement. I still want that post, perhaps more than ever. And since, thanks to Brendon, I've just announced my plans to marry, I think I should be nominated." The minute he agreed to award her the prestigious post, she would tell him it was all a joke, despite Brendon's threats.

Emerson gritted his teeth and folded his arms across his chest. He surveyed Savannah for a long moment. "You really do want that position, don't you?"

She sighed. "I'm beginning to think I'd do almost anything to get it." Her voice ended on a genuine quaver.

Emerson grinned, and his mouth twisted wryly. "All right, Savannah," he said, putting his drink aside, "you've made your point. But I warn you, I'm not going to make it easy for you. If you want that position, you're going to have to present the most stable image possible, and that means not too many surprises in either your personal or professional life. You will also have to succeed in implementing the Paradise project and work well with your peers here."

"Thank you." She breathed a sigh of relief. "I won't let you down, I promise." Now she would tell him it was a joke, and they'd all have a good laugh and maybe share another round of drinks.

"I'm not finished yet," Emerson broke in grimly. Her head jerked up. Her grandfather's silvery brows lowered warningly. "Since you and Brendon have done such a good job of convincing me of your devotion to one another, there's one more condition."

Tension formed a tight knot in her stomach. Oh, rubbish! She knew they should have quit while they were ahead. "What is it?" she queried warily, perspiration dampening her palms.

"If you truly want the position, you must marry before I retire," Emerson said calmly. Silence fell, giving the drawing room the cheerfulness of a tomb. "Fail to fulfill any one of the aforementioned terms and you will be assured a vice-presidency and a place on the board of directors—and that is all, permanently."

Brendon and Savannah stood motionless. She didn't know what was going through his mind, but she vowed never to play another reckless prank as long as she lived.

Obviously satisfied with the results of their talk, Emerson was the first to speak. "If you two young people will excuse me, I think I'll go up and dress for dinner. We're having company. Savannah, will you and your beau be joining me here this evening?"

Brendon sent her a glittering glance. "Thank you, sir, but Savannah and I must decline the invitation now that we have important plans to make," he interjected smoothly.

"I'll see you tomorrow morning then, Savannah. Perhaps we can drive in to the office together and discuss your wedding then." Emerson left the room, closing the doors to the drawing room behind him. She and Brendon stared at one another without speaking.

Finally she broke the silence. "Well, that's what I get for trying to put one over on the master," she remarked.

Not only had Emerson evidently figured out she was bluffing, he'd also taught her a lesson she'd remember for the rest of her life.

"Never place a wager you're not prepared to lose," Brendon admonished, staring thoughtfully off into space. He glanced at her, and his mouth lifted in a wry curve.

She forced down an impulse to hurl something at him. "How nice you're such a good loser," she retorted sarcastically, running a hand through her hair. How could he be so calm after what they'd just been through? The man must have nerves of steel!

"There are two sides to every coin." He shrugged. "This time we caught the downside."

"Remind me to nominate you for poker-playing hellion of the year," she retorted. "Don't you know when to cut your losses and get out?"

"When I want to." Laughter rumbled low in his throat. He stepped closer and ran a hand up her arm. She jerked away, still furious. "What you need is a good dinner and a nice bottle of wine," he prescribed. "Perhaps when you've relaxed you'll be able to analyze our situation calmly."

"And then what? Marry you to gain the presidency?" she asked with contempt. "No thanks!" She threw open the drawing room doors. Brendon followed her out, his hands in his pockets. She gritted her teeth, infuriated by his unshakable calm. Her boots made an angry staccato sound on the parquet floor.

When they reached the foyer, Brendon grabbed her wrist. She saw Emerson's housekeeper arranging a vase of flowers in the background. If she and Brendon had an argument, her grandfather was sure to hear of it. She forced a smile and followed Brendon obediently through the door, down the front steps, and into the courtyard. "Let go of me!" she demanded, as soon as they were out of sight and earshot of the house.

"And have you spill your guts to Emerson at the first available opportunity? Not a chance, Savannah!" Brendon stated boldly. "You're coming with me."

She dug in her heels. No one was going to tell her what

to do. When she didn't follow, he halted on the rough cobblestone walk, his eyes glowing with an angry warning. The cool January breeze lent a ruddiness to his cheeks. "I'm not going anywhere with you," she stated between gritted teeth.

He shrugged and smiled. "Fine. Then we'll both stay for dinner with Emerson and his guests. That ought to be interesting."

She knew he meant every word he said. She knew, too, that she'd never get through a social evening with the two combative men. Still she stubbornly refused to go with him.

He sighed and rolled his eyes heavenward, then began to roam the well-landscaped grounds. He glanced inquiringly toward the small one-story carriage house behind the mansion. It was surrounded by a thick grove of trees and masses of winter-blooming camellias. "Is that where you live?"

"Since I've been back." She shoved her hands into the pockets of her blazer, wanting to stay angry at him because it was her best defense. In reality, she knew she was at least as responsible as he was for her current predicament. "It's much nicer than an apartment, and I have all the privacy I need." Her tone was short and defensive.

Brendon gave her a disapproving look. "Nice for a spinster," he muttered.

Savannah's temper flared. "Are you finished?"

He grinned lazily, and from the way he looked at her, she knew he was thoroughly enjoying her bad temper. "I don't know why you're so angry at me," he said. "I did everything you asked."

"And more." Heat flared in her cheeks as she recalled the way he'd held her against him and trailed his fingertips over her arms. "Needless to say, Brendon, you overplayed your part!" She spun on her heel and stalked to the curb. The sooner she got him into his Mercedes and off McLean property, the sooner she'd be free.

"Now, Savannah . . ." He caught her arm and brought her up short. Her breasts brushed his chest. She pulled back.

"Don't 'now Savannah' me!" she exclaimed hoarsely.

"You've gotten me into a terrible mess! Emerson thinks you want to marry me!"

"Maybe I do." His voice was low and enigmatic. "I can certainly think of worse fates." She stared at him in wide-eyed disbelief. He quirked his brows rakishly and grinned, and she knew he was teasing her.

"Stop joking!" she admonished severely. "If you hadn't gotten so carried away and said you were going to make me your wife, we wouldn't be in this mess!"

"If you're going to throw stones, Savannah," he said, "let's start with the meeting in my office. Besides, if you hadn't looked so guilty and indecisive the moment we walked through your grandfather's door, it probably wouldn't have been necessary to mention marriage. As it was, it was the only move I could think of on the spur of the moment that would convince him we weren't bluffing. And that was the objective, wasn't it? To shake your grandfather into an awareness of what he was asking of you?"

"Well, we did that all right, and he likes his original idea just fine!" she raged. "Oh, for heaven's sake!"

Brendon's laughter was low and husky. She was sorely tempted to slap his face. "Would you just go home?"

"I'd like to, but you won't come with me," Brendon teased. "Be reasonable." His voice lowered cajolingly. "After what just happened, we need to talk. And your grandfather's front yard is not the best place to hold a strategy session."

She glanced at the windows along the front of the mansion. Brendon was right. Someone might see or overhear them. And she could hardly blame him alone for the fiasco. She was the one who had thought up the prank and enlisted his help. If it had backfired on her, she had herself to blame first. If anything, she should admire his composure in the face of so much disaster. He couldn't want to be engaged to her any more than she wanted to be engaged to him.

"Have dinner with me," he urged softly. She looked away, exasperated and confused. "Like it or not, we're in this mess together, Savannah."

She turned warily to him. Why was he behaving so reasonably? It would have been so much easier if she could have stayed angry. "I suppose we do need to talk," she conceded.

"Then it's settled." Brendon took her arm, opened the gate, and led her to his Mercedes. "We'll take my car." She stared at him recalcitrantly. "You're too distracted to drive," he explained. "I'll bring you home early, I promise. Think of the gasoline we'll save."

"In the interest of conserving energy, I'll ride with you," she said. Her mind whirled with conflicting emotions, but Brendon was right; they did need to talk—privately.

She slid into the plush seat. He shut the passenger door and slid into the driver's seat. "I'll pay," she decided.

"If it's all the same to you, I'd rather go to my place," he said, cutting her objections short. He started the engine and directed the car onto the street, still not glancing at her. "I'd rather not chance any of what we say being overheard. At least not until we've figured a graceful way out of this mess—one that won't forfeit you the presidency of McLean. You can buy me dinner some other time."

Savannah remained silent. Under normal circumstances she would have refused his suggestion. But this was a very unusual situation. "All right," she finally said, feeling as if she'd fallen into a silken trap. "But let's make it an early evening."

He grinned wickedly. "Afraid to be alone with me?"

She forced down her rising temper. "Lots of work to do tomorrow, that's all." And she wanted the prank over as soon as possible.

"The Paradise project?" he guessed.

"Mmmhmm." Savannah's thoughts drifted to Emerson's triple criteria for the presidency of his firm. "I asked for and received complete control of the condominium project our firm is building on Edisto Island."

"Sounds interesting," Brendon murmured distractedly.

"It should be." She sighed. "I'm making a lot of changes on it. And we're going to have to do a lot of additional construction to meet the slated April first opening date."

Brendon directed the Mercedes into a Sloane-built condominium project off Lockwood Drive and parked at the rear of the complex. His two-story town house was Colonial in style, made of red brick with white trim, and featured glossy black shutters. Inside it was as opulently luxurious as his office, but all male and more middle America than nouveau chic. The living room, dining room, and small galley kitchen were spotlessly clean. The plush leather sofa and armchairs, heavy oak furniture, and crowded bookshelves spoke well of his taste. "I like your town house," she said. "Did you decorate it yourself?"

"Yes."

"What about your office?" She circled the room slowly, deliberately putting space between them.

"I had a professional do that, someone who works for my firm." He strolled closer, his eyes never leaving hers. His hands loosely circled her waist. "Which do you like better?"

"This."

"So do I."

Feeling uncomfortable under his close scrutiny, she walked over to his bookcases. Judging by the contents, his life was long on work and short on play. Although there were many business, legal, and construction texts, he owned few novels.

Brendon watched her for a moment, then walked over to the phone and ordered a picnic-basket supper from a local catering service. "Make yourself at home," he advised pleasantly. "There are some cold drinks in the refrigerator. I've got a business call to make. I'll do it upstairs."

When he returned ten minutes later, he was wearing a soft ecru sweater and matching corduroy jeans. A beguiling flutter began in her stomach, which intensified when she noticed that he had shaved and brushed his hair. The scent of his cologne engulfed her as he sat beside her on the couch. Did he really have seduction on his mind or was it her imagination? "Our dinner should be here soon," he said. "Would you like me to build a fire?"

"If you want to." Her mouth was dry.

"I do." He patted her knee lightly and crossed to the fireplace. She watched him stack paper and logs, light a

match, and ignite the fire. Her heart raced in the silence,
but he seemed completely immersed in his task. In desper-
ation she grabbed the afternoon paper and unfolded it. The
words blurred before her eyes as he walked past her to the
stereo. The conduciveness of their surroundings and his
relaxed mood only escalated her panic. The couch was too
soft, too deep, too long, too perfect for seduction. There
were too many throw pillows within easy reach. He was
too attractive, too sensually skilled. He was too much of a
temptation.

Part of her, she realized, wanted to make love with Brendon Sloane. Part of her worried she wouldn't measure up
to his expectations. She knew it was too soon to consider
such intimacy. She didn't make love to a man casually. In
fact, she hadn't ever made love with anyone except her
husband.

Still her thoughts strayed to the corded muscles beneath
his soft sweater, his lean hips and taut stomach. What would
that body feel like over hers? How gently would his hands
caress her?

A click sounded, and the room was filled with up-tempo
rock music. She relaxed. It was hardly music to seduce by,
unless of course he knew her tastes, and he didn't.

"Here, make yourself useful." Brendon tossed her a tablecloth and a bundle of linen napkins from the lower cabinet
of the dining room hutch. "Spread that out before the fire."

He walked over and shoved the coffee table to one side
with his knee. Wordlessly he tossed throw pillows onto the
floor. Then the doorbell rang, and his eyes lit up. "Dinner!"

He brought a split oak basket into the room. Delving
into it, they discovered roast chicken; crusty French bread;
wedges of Brie, Edam, cheddar, and Gruyère; apples,
grapes, and sweet ripe pears. By mutual agreement he opened
a bottle of wine while she sliced and divided the roast chicken.
Her thoughts turned to the dramatic afternoon. "Why so
glum?" Brendon asked, biting into a wedge of Brie.

"I was thinking about the presidency. I want it so badly,
and now it seems further out of my reach than ever before.
My grandfather knows there's no way I'm going to marry

anyone again in the near future, never mind beating that
April first time frame by tripping merrily to the altar with
you."

Brendon sipped his wine slowly. "Was your first marriage that miserable?"

She sighed wearily. The fire, the meal, and his company
made her feel relaxed and reflective. "If you'd asked me
the day I married Keith, I would have sworn we would be
married until death do us part. Now all I remember is the
fighting."

"What'd you argue about?"

She shrugged, staring into the flames. "My career,
mostly," she said softly. "I had to work long, hard hours.
He did, too, so at first there was no problem. But when my
career took off, he started making demands. Most of them
were outrageous, and I see in retrospect that he intended to
make them impossible to meet. What had been an equal part-
nership turned into a fight for domination. He was always
yelling about the laundry or an errand I hadn't had time to do,
or worse yet hadn't done properly." Savannah tried hard to
keep the hurt out of her voice. "I can't cook." She laughed
abruptly. "What once was a family joke became a major crisis. Eventually I stopped trying to please him, and he walked
out." Tears welled up unexpectedly, and she dashed them away
with a grimace, aware that Brendon was watching her every
movement. Yet she wasn't able to face him.

"I'm sorry," he said softly, touching her shoulder.

She covered his hand lightly with her own, then moved
it away. She didn't want his sympathy. There was no point
in indulging in her hurt. "It happened. It's over. But I've
still got my work."

"Is that why you want the presidency so badly?" Brendon
plucked a green grape and slid it beteeen her lips. She caught
it with her teeth, and the warmth of her mouth accidentally
closed over his finger and thumb. He prolonged the sensual
contact, then drew back. New lights smoldered in his eyes.

She forced herself to remember his question. "The firm
has needed new blood for years," she replied in a low, husky
voice laced with new tension. "John Crawford is a wonderful

man, but he's very conservative and short-sighted, afraid to take chances. If McLean Development is under his direction, it will continue to decline or stagnate. I've got a responsibility both to myself and to the people our company employs to do everything possible to make the firm prosper."

Wordlessly he tucked a strand of hair behind her ear. His steady gaze mesmerized her. She observed the way the firelight played on the rugged contours of his face. His gaze lingered over the soft swell of her breasts before returning to her face. Ripples of awareness swept over her, making her tingle from head to foot. How had she ever allowed a mere practical joke to become such an untenable situation?

"I guess I'll talk to my grandfather tomorrow," she said.

"No matter how fickle it might make you seem?" he asked casually. "Face it, Savannah, you can't confess without destroying your credibility. Emerson will label you flighty and indecisive, and a businesswoman can't afford even the suggestion of either trait."

"True."

"Besides which, my reputation's at stake, too. If Emerson or his housekeeper mentions what transpired this afternoon, the news will be all over town within hours."

"I'm sorry I dragged you into this." She sighed dispiritedly. "Had I known how it was going to turn out, I never would have asked."

"That's all beside the point now, isn't it?" he said impatiently.

She gaped at him in amazement. Surely he didn't expect the situation to continue indefinitely! "Brendon, I'm not good at deception," she warned.

"Well, sweetheart, you'd better start practicing." He began picking up the remains of the meal. She watched as he folded the tablecloth neatly. "Because this poker game has just started."

She stared at him incredulously. "We have to tell Emerson the truth, Brendon, and the sooner the better. It's our only way out of this predicament. Granted, it won't be easy—"

"We're not going to confess." His voice cut into hers like a knife. He rose and helped her wordlessly to her feet. His eyes glinted with unexpected humor. "Personally, I like the idea of having McLean Development's new president for my wife, at least in theory. You have to admit our engagement would give the local good-old-boys a much-needed jolt. They've had a hard time accepting me, both socially and professionally. They've had even more trouble accepting my success."

So Emerson had said. "You're planning to use your relationship with me to elevate your social position here?"

Brendon sat down on the sofa and calmly adjusted a pillow behind his back. She took a chair opposite him, crossed her legs, and pulled down the hem of her skirt. "Why not?" he countered lightly. "You used me to raise Emerson's consciousness."

Panic crowded her thoughts, but she forced herself to remain calm. Obviously he hadn't forgiven her for offending him earlier in his office. Now she had to talk her way out of it. "I'm sorry if I affronted you. I only came to you because I considered you a friend."

"Well, now I want a favor from you." He studied her carefully. "How much do you know about the history of the Edisto Island project?"

"Not much. When I arrived in Charleston, the property had already been bought and most of the foundations were already laid," she admitted, surprised by the abrupt change of subject.

"And Emerson hasn't told you anything?" Brendon's fingers drummed restlessly on the arm of the sofa.

"No."

"Then maybe it's time you were treated to some cold hard facts." He rose and began to pace the room restlessly. "Maybe then you'll understand why I'm so determined to milk this engagement for all it's worth. When I said I owed Emerson one, I meant it. We've maintained an avid dislike of one another these past five years, and generally with very good reason. The competition between our firms has been cutthroat down to the wire. The last in a long line of skirmishes was over that Edisto Island property your firm is developing. That was mine, Savannah. I found it, wooed the owners into selling, did all the legwork, and had gone almost as far as closing the deal before my loan was mysteriously pulled by the local bank. Emerson stepped in and bought the property before I could get financing from anyone else. Coincidence? Knowing the good-old-boy network he operates in, I doubt it."

Brendon stopped pacing and faced her. "Naturally the past month and a half I've been curious about this new granddaughter of his, since it was no secret you were determined to take over the family firm and well qualified to do so, too. I might even have started dating you eventually to find out more about you. I admit it crossed my mind, which was why I chased you down to the powder room that first day, once I'd figured out who you were and caught you staring my way more than once. I didn't count on you coming to me and laying such an outrageous scheme in my lap. But as Emerson said to me on the day he bought the Edisto Island property, 'Son, you really couldn't expect me to pass up such a sweet deal, now could you? Not when all the groundwork's already been laid?' So you see, Savannah, it's history repeating itself, and this time it's oh so right!"

Sickening dread filled Savannah's stomach. Brendon's unexpected revelation complicated the situation enormously. Obviously by coming to him with her original plan to secure the presidency, she'd unknowingly walked straight into the lion's den! Now Brendon was in a position to exact revenge for an injustice she'd had nothing to do with.

Brendon's expression was taut with rage. If everything he'd told her was true—and knowing some of Emerson's friends, she could easily believe it was—he had every right to be angry. But he didn't have cause to use her.

Savannah stood. "What do you want from me?" Her legs were shaking. Her jaw was rigid with resentment.

"An engagement," Brendon said simply. He smiled, and the tension in his shoulders eased. His dark eyes traversed her leisurely from head to toe. "I want to give Emerson a real run for his money and make him think you and I are seriously intending to marry."

CHAPTER
Six

"You can't honestly think I would pretend to be your fiancée," Savannah asserted.

Brendon favored her with a lazy grin. "That's what you led Emerson to believe."

"My mistake!" she said, her voice grating. She grabbed up her handbag and started for the door, with Brendon stalking her step for furious step. The palm of his hand pressed flat against the front door, preventing her from opening it. She whirled to face him. His arm outstretched, he leaned over her. A muscle worked in his cheek.

"There's something you'd better understand, Savannah," he said in a low, threatening voice. "When I start something, I'm in for the duration, win or lose. And in this case you are too."

"Well, I've got news for you," she shouted. "I quit!"

"Like hell you do! You're not the only one with a reputation at stake," he said grimly. "Just how far do you think I'd get in this town if word got out you were dragging me around like some pet on a leash!"

"I don't know and I don't care." She whirled and yanked on the door again. When it still wouldn't open, she tossed her purse aside and used both hands to pull. Still it wouldn't budge. Brendon towered above her, one long arm still fastened languidly in place, the bunched muscles of his forearm taut.

"Finished with the high drama?" he drawled.

Savannah couldn't prevent the expletive that hissed through her teeth. She glared at him, hating his complacent expression. "The thought of continuing our liaison under such deceptive terms really doesn't upset you, does it?" she said with some calmness.

His white teeth flashed in a devastating smile. "I can think of a few fringe benefits, not the least of which is spending time alone with you."

She gave the door another savage yank, but her efforts to escape failed miserably and she flushed with anger. She noted Brendon's amusement with chagrin. "My grandfather was right. You *are* a scoundrel," she accused in a very low voice.

He laughed deep in his throat. "Ah, yes, but a clever one—one you enjoyed kissing very much this afternoon. One who would like to kiss you again."

She laughed humorlessly. "Not if you were the last man on earth!" Unfortunately, the insult sounded more like a challenge. His brows rose.

"As far as you're concerned, from this moment forward I am the *only* man on this earth. So you'd better start practicing your openly adoring looks."

"The only thing I feel for you is contempt!"

He grinned, shaking his head. "You're pure passion, Savannah. And one day I'm going to discover it all."

"Never!" She tried to push past.

"Oh yes, Savannah, I will."

"I won't let you touch me."

He mocked her blatantly. "We'll see about that." Without

warning he clamped a hand on her waist and pulled her inexorably closer. "Think of it this way, Savannah. Sooner or later someone is going to have to give up or give in. And it's not going to be us." He sighed deeply, surveying her with a slow appreciative gaze. "In all likelihood we would have been spending time together anyway."

Before she could protest, he had cupped her face with an open palm. If he had tried to force her into submission, it would have been appallingly easy to slap his face. But his lips fluttered lightly across hers, brushed her mouth tenuously, whispered across her temple. Despite her anger, a shiver of physical awareness rocked her.

She had to fight the attraction she felt for him. It was purely physical. She would not indulge it. "I won't continue this engagement," she stated flatly, dismayed at the quaver in her voice.

His lips brushed hers fleetingly again. "Yes, you will, if I have to spend the entire night persuading you. I want you, Savannah. I have since the first moment we met."

"I was a fool ever to let you kiss me," she declared, hating herself for her weakness.

"Yes, you were," he agreed softly. "And you're even more foolish if you think you can ignore the attraction between us now."

She pushed at his chest. She could feel the fierce beating of his heart under her fingertips. "I don't care what you want," she whispered. "I never intended any of it to go this far."

He regarded her contemplatively, then shrugged. "Have it your own way. But start preparing yourself for the unexpected." He swung her up into his arms and cradled her resolutely in his powerful grip. The softness of wool was beneath her face, the steel of his shoulder under that. "Ten to one we're going to be encountering a lot of snags before this scam is through. It's crucial that you learn to improvise."

"Put me down!" she demanded furiously. Who did he think he was, manhandling her that way!

"Gladly," Brendon murmured as he moved languidly up

the stairs. "You haven't seen my bedroom, have you?" he inquired solicitously.

Her pulse had tripled. "If you carry me to your bedroom, I will never forgive you," she said through gritted teeth. Reluctantly she wound one arm around his neck to keep from falling. The other hand pushed furiously at his shoulder.

He grinned, his low, sexy laugh contradicting her words. "You mean if I don't make it to my bed, you'll never forgive me. Come on, Savannah, where's your memory?" He stopped, shifting her slightly in his possessive embrace. His voice lowered seductively, and she knew the rakehell in him had emerged full force. "You know what happened between us this afternoon. Aren't you the least bit curious to find out if the fireworks will explode again?" His face changed stonily when she refused to reply. "Or was your reaction to me all part of the deal?" he wondered aloud. "A calculated enticement to get me to help put Emerson through his paces."

Too late, she realized he thought she had ruthlessly used him. Now he was about to extract his revenge. Was turnabout fair play? Did she trust him not to go too far?

Seconds later he reached the top of the carpeted staircase and strode determinedly down the hall, past what looked like a much-used home office and into the huge master bedroom. A king-sized bed covered with a satiny comforter in muted champagne brown seemed to fill the room. An armoire stood against one wall. A bedstand, mirrored gentleman's dresser, and a large chest were all in the same heavy oak.

"Okay, Brendon, fun and games are over," she said in a bored tone. "You've had your joke. I get the message. I will never use you as a player in a practical joke again."

He smiled. "You're right about that much."

He tossed her onto the satiny spread. She stifled a gasp and the urge to call out for help. It suddenly seemed expedient to offer him a promise. "I swear I'll never ask another favor of you as long as I live. I'll do all the explaining to my grandfather myself, spare you any further involvement."

"Oh no." Brendon moved lithely down to cover her body with his own. "You're not getting off that easy, Savannah McLean. Not by a long shot. You didn't really think I'd let myself be used that way without expecting *some* payment in return, did you? I'm not an escort for hire, Savannah."

He trapped her face between his hands. A moment passed as they studied one another warily. Eventually his breathing slowed and hers stretched out to match his own ragged cadence. The world seemed to narrow to include just the two of them. His sensual aggression was no longer a teasing punishment for indignities she had inflicted on his pride. It was desire, hot and pulsing. She hadn't felt so aroused in years, not since the early days of her marriage, and even then it hadn't been so potent or compelling. No, she decided, considering the circumstances of their involvement, this bedroom scene was not something she would be wise to pursue.

She tried to rise, but he held her easily with his full weight. "Brendon, don't." Afraid he would see how amorous her inclinations were, she tried desperately to reason her way out of the embrace. "My boots will ruin the fabric."

"There are three other comforters in that hope chest at the foot of the bed," he murmured, tickling her neck with his warm, fragrant breath. His lips nuzzled her hair. "But if you insist on worrying..."

Placing one hand firmly across her waist, he leaned over to tug off one black suede boot. Despite her exasperated protests, he managed to remove the other one, as well. His own shoes fell to the floor beside hers. "There—all done." Languidly he moved back up to cover her body with his own.

There was another breathless pause as he drew out the passionate threat, obviously enjoying himself. Savannah was not amused. "Okay," she said finally, trying to inject glibness back into the casual warring between them. "Using you to rile Emerson was a mistake. I'm sorry."

"You admit it?" He seemed to be searching for more than an apology.

"I swear it." She affected a tight, conciliatory smile.

Could he feel how rapidly her pulse was beating? Did he know how very little of it was due to apprehension? "Brendon, you're trying my patience."

"And you have no idea at all what you've done to mine!" He glanced speculatively down at her. His muscular frame rippled as he gave a contented sigh. Reaction spread through her, chilling and warming her simultaneously. "Do you know how long it's been since a woman even remotely piqued my interest? No one's ever dragged me on a tour of her grandfather's mansion or asked me to pose as an unsuitable beau!"

"I apologized for that!"

"Who's complaining?" he said sarcastically. "I'm flattered, Savannah; flattered you chose me. Flattered we're going to be spending so much time together."

Her lips clamped together stubbornly, and she stared up at him in vexation. "I wouldn't date you now if you were the last man in Charleston!"

"Now, Savannah," he murmured, playfully nuzzling her neck, "don't make promises you won't want to keep."

If only she were still wearing her black suede boots. She longed to kick him with something that had more impact than a stocking-covered toe.

His mouth traced her chin. He studied her parted lips. "Poor darling," he crooned. "I don't think you realize even yet the enormity of what you've done."

His mouth closed over hers, probing, parting her lips. His tongue caressed the edge of her teeth and slid further into her mouth. Panicking both at the conduciveness of their surroundings as well as his leisurely exploration of her lips, she tried to twist free of his grip. Brendon laughed deep in his throat and settled more heavily against her. "However, I'm all too willing to drive the lesson home." Warm lips trailed teasingly up the slope of her neck to her chin and moved languidly to the delicate lobe of her ear.

"Brendon, for heaven's sake!" With difficulty, she partially freed herself from his embrace and pushed up onto her elbows, her hair falling in disarray around her face and shoulders.

Brendon drew back and studied her with open amusement. "For a woman who came to me this afternoon and begged me to come to dinner and at the very least upset Emerson McLean, you're not being very cooperative now."

"This wasn't part of the package." She scrambled toward the other side of the bed over the slick and slippery comforter. When her soles hit the floor, he reached up lazily, grabbed her arm, and pulled her back to the center of the bed. "I think you make a most delightful package," he said. Her immediate resistance only succeeded in getting her back against the pillows, his weight on top of her. He overcame her struggles effortlessly and pinned both her arms above her head. "The kiss in my office this afternoon was at your leisure, Savannah," he said softly. "Now we're going to do it at mine."

He surveyed her boldly. His free hand lifted her chin. She felt a momentary panic as his mouth descended slowly to hers, but it dissolved under the spiraling sensations generated by his touch. This time there was no hesitation in his embrace, no tentative exploration, no slow, subtle plea for her response. This time he took and aroused, pulling her deep within a whirlpool of desire.

Sensations she had been trying hard to ignore came rushing relentlessly over her. The warm feeling of his chest over hers; the soft knit of his sweater; the scent of his aftershave, so pleasant and male; the gentleness of his open palm as he caressed her from waist to hip. She tasted the wine on his breath and felt the increasing pressure of his knee as he slowly but surely edged her legs apart. At last he was nestled against her in the most intimate way possible. The urge to flee ebbed dangerously.

The barrier of their clothing did little to hide his insistent masculine desire. She melted reluctantly against him, noticing without wanting to how well their bodies molded to one another, despite the difference in their height, the width of his shoulders compared to hers, the sloping curve of her hips compared to the taut leanness of his. She recalled his humor the first time they'd had dinner, his sympathy when she'd talked about her failed marriage. She remembered that they'd been friends before they'd become adversaries.

Brendon's grip on her wrists lessened. She knew she should insist he take her home, but the sweetness of his kiss combined with the passion he was generating kept her in place. Her arms moved around his neck, and slid across his shoulders as she plunged her hands into his thick hair. The darkness was a velvet cloud around them, enticing her to further intimacies. When his lips drifted to the curve of her throat, his fingers to the slope of her breast, she did not resist. She needed to feel cherished, cared for, desired. Until this moment she hadn't realized how much.

Nimble masculine fingers unfastened the buttons of her blouse. His hand slid across the smooth skin of her abdomen, pausing at the curving underside of her breast. His lips brushed her collarbone and drifted down to the edge of her lacy white bra. Expertly he undid the front clasp and opened her to his sensual regard.

Suddenly she realized what she was doing, allowing, almost asking to happen. Reality returned with a crash. She had never spent the night with a man other than her husband. She needed love and mutual commitment before letting her feelings culminate in an act of physical intimacy. Instinctively she drew her hands across her breasts.

"You're so sweet, so soft." He brushed her arms and hands aside and kept them there when she tried to shield herself. "Let me see you, Savannah," he whispered in a voice of softest velvet. His lambent gaze drifted to her lips, shoulders, breasts. She saw only tenderness in his regard. "Let me touch you, love you. I won't hurt you."

His lips brushed hers once again and lingered seductively. His masculine fingertips circled taut rose satin tips and traced the fullness of creamy white flesh. "I won't do anything you don't agree to." His lips moved commandingly over hers, then more gently.

She had no will to halt the gentle, sensual persuasion. It was so much easier to surrender to the desire he had evoked than to think about consequences, the future, her responsibility to herself.

His softly parted lips brushed the rosy tip of her breast

and traced the hollow in between. Over and over his lips
caressed her. She tried to breathe deeply, tried to think, but
it was no use. She was caught in his sensual snare, a willing
participant in whatever passionate folly he might commit.
She wanted him so badly she ached.

It hadn't been that way with her husband. Sometimes
she'd felt a certain urgency, followed by a lingering regret
after they'd made love. But she'd never felt this overwhelming need. After so short an acquaintance, she never would
have allowed Keith to haul her off to his bedroom, partially
undress her and caress her intimately. Months had passed
before they'd gone to bed, and then only after they'd been
married. Now guilt permeated her consciousness, slowly
but surely destroying her ardor.

A tear slid from the corner of her tightly shut eye, then
another and another. Brendon stopped as abruptly as if he'd
been shot. He traced the salty moisture on her face. She sat
up and pulled the edges of her blouse together. She felt like
such a fool. "You haven't been with anyone else since your
divorce, have you?" he asked softly.

Her throat constricted with emotion, she slowly shook
her head. He paused. She could hear the rough, slightly
shallow cadence of his breathing and knew without a doubt
that he must feel thoroughly frustrated. "Were you thinking
of your ex-husband now?" he asked.

He must have seen the confirmation in her face before
she could deny it. With an oath he rose from the bed and
stalked to the window, pulled back the drape, and stood
staring out into the dark night. Finally he turned toward her.
She couldn't read the emotion in his eyes. "Do you still
love him? Is that it?" he demanded, his voice low.

"No." She glanced away. Her fingers traced an intricate
pattern on the quilted spread. How could she explain the
confused welter of emotions flooding her at that moment
without sounding like even more of a fool? How could she
tell him about the way Keith had rejected and belittled her,
how he had shaken her confidence—professionally, sexually, and emotionally—until she had almost believed she

wasn't an attractive or intelligent woman capable of loving and being loved in return.

"Brendon, I don't want to discuss this." She slid off the bed. At first she couldn't locate her boots. With trembling fingers she refastened her bra.

He strode back to her. "Damn it, Savannah, you can't leave me like this, wondering what I've done. Did I hurt you?"

Numbly she shook her head. He towered over her. "Then why the tears?" he questioned softly, persistently.

She swallowed, realizing he wasn't likely to accept anything but the truth. She gritted her teeth and dashed away the tears and the rest of her pride. "Because it was never any good between Keith and me." She swallowed, turning away from his probing gaze. "Not as good as it was with you and me just now. And I wondered—" She swallowed, fighting back a fresh onslaught of emotion.

"Go on." His voice was quieter, less tense.

She sighed tremulously, relieved to be able to tell someone finally. "I wondered if Keith would have loved me more if I'd been good in bed." There; it was out. Now Brendon knew, too.

He was silent, staring down at her. Ever so gently he extended a hand to hers. After a moment's hesitation, Savannah took it. His clasp felt warm and comforting. He pulled her to her feet and against his chest so that her head rested on his shoulder. Slowly he stroked her back. "He left you because of something that happened in bed?" Brendon asked incredulously.

"Or didn't happen." She wound her arms about his waist. More tears flowed, tears she had held back for the better part of a year. She leaned into Brendon, savoring his strength and compassion. Because she wasn't looking at him, it was easier to continue. "Neither of us was very experienced when we got married. I knew only what he brought to the marriage, and he—he didn't teach me much. Later, when it became apparent that he was less than satisfied with my skills, I read some how-to manuals." She felt herself blushing fire-engine red, but she went on determinedly. "That turned him off even more. He accused me of being a sexual misfit, an incompetent. He said if I had been half the woman I thought I was, I would have been able to please him without even trying, that the skills would have come naturally and I just didn't have them." Her throat tightened, and she finished in a tortured whisper. "I tried. I swear I did. But I just couldn't please him. After a while it seemed simpler to stop trying."

Brendon gripped her shoulders and studied her face. She tried to evade his scrutiny. Then, with fresh courage, she met his eyes. "I assume your ex-husband got some satisfaction out of the experience," Brendon stated angrily.

Heat flooded her cheeks. "Yes."

"And left you unsatisfied?"

She glanced away, glad for the cover of darkness. "Brendon, please . . ."

"Today in my office, when I asked you to be the aggressor, were you bothered by my request?" His tone was curt, underlined with a new tension she couldn't identify.

She felt herself blush crimson again. Why not admit it? What difference did it make? "I enjoyed it," she murmured. Her throat was so dry she felt as if she were speaking around a mouthful of cotton.

"Good." He sighed as if he had been relieved of a tremendous burden. "I did, too. And I'm sorry about just now. I shouldn't have demanded so much so soon. You seem to have an unusual effect on me. And for the record, Savannah, your ex-husband must have been a clumsy, arrogant fool. Because you're sexy and skilled as hell." His praise made her glow with pleasure.

They drove home in silence. Savannah was exhausted and felt drained after expressing herself so openly and revealing so much to Brendon, who now seemed oddly distracted. He insisted on walking her from the car to the carriage house.

She located her keys and unlocked the door. Blocking his entrance, she said, "Good night, Brendon."

He grinned. "No good night kiss?"

"You already had that."

"And more," he teased. "How about breakfast tomorrow? Can we meet before you go to the office?"

She shook her head. She wanted to see him again, but not until she had cleared up the misunderstanding with her grandfather. "I can't. I've got to talk to Emerson. Don't worry." She laughed at Brendon's concerned glance. "You'll be off the hook before you know it."

"I take it that means you've decided to confess, despite my advice to the contrary?" His brows arched.

She ignored his dismay. "It was a juvenile ploy. I see that now." She sighed, thinking how differently she'd envisioned the drawing room scene: Emerson admitting he'd been wrong to insist that she would be happier married; Emerson agreeing to give her a clear shot at the company presidency, no strings attached. "I'm going to clear the slate, accept full responsibility for the prank, and go on. My grandfather may understand and sympathize with my mistakes." She thought of Emerson's regrets about his own failed marriage and the fact that he had never been able to reconcile with her grandmother or give up the family firm's demands. "Ambition is one trait we share indubitably."

She turned toward her door, but Brendon caught her arm. "I'd still like to come over for breakfast," he insisted softly. "I'll help you talk to Emerson."

She shook her head again. Brendon was dangerously attractive, and she didn't want to tempt the fates again. But he drew her completely into the warm cradle of his muscular arms. "I'll see you in the morning," he repeated, kissing her brow.

"That sounds suspiciously like an order," she retorted, her temper rising. Couldn't he ever take no for an answer?

"If you're wondering about my culinary preferences," he went on with an audacious wink, "I like my bacon crisp, my eggs sunny side up, my coffee hot as Hades and twice as strong. You owe me a meal, darling. I'm collecting at dawn."

But, Brendon's request reminded Savannah all too clearly

of her ex-husband's often-petulant demands. Her desire dissipated into the coldness of an unwelcome memory. She'd vowed not to repeat her past mistake by molding herself to someone else's perception of what a wife or a girl friend or even a business associate ought to be. It was a promise she was fully determined to keep. "Mr. Sloane, I might owe you one small favor as promised, if you haven't already been repaid. But I'm not about to turn into an overly attentive man-pleasing Southern belle." She had a company presidency to obtain. And at the moment the major force standing in her way, aside from her grandfather's old-fashioned beliefs, was Brendon.

"You're sure now," he teased in a parody of a thick Southern drawl. "I can be mighty persuasive when I set my mind to it."

"Show up here for breakfast, Brendon," she said sweetly, "and you may just get your wish—one cup of coffee meant to burn." The door slammed. From the other side she heard the low drift of masculine laughter before Brendon strolled away, whistling.

CHAPTER
Seven

SAVANNAH DREAMED THAT a hurricane had blown inland
and descended over the roof of the small one-story carriage
house. The wind and rain pounded incessantly, growing
steadily to a formidable pitch, until at last she was forced
to abandon her restless sleep and pull the pillow over her
head. Finally she realized someone was knocking on the
door.

"All right," she grumbled, pushing wispy tendrils from
her eyes. Wearily she sat up and gazed at the light filtering
beneath the drapes. It was morning. The digital clock beside
her bed indicated it was almost six. If she hadn't been
disturbed, she could have slept another hour.

She rose and pulled a fluffy white chenille robe over her
floor-length plum-color nightgown. Her bare feet scooted
across the cold parquet floor to the dusky rose-gray-and-blue
floral rug decorating the living room. She leaned against

the door. "Yes?" She cursed her lack of peephole and the waviness of the leaded glass. "Who is it?" she muttered grouchily. "What do you want?"

"Guess."

The low voice was achingly familiar. It had haunted her dreams. "Brendon, what are you doing here?" she demanded with exasperation. She wasn't going to let him in no matter how much he cajoled, demanded, or pleaded.

"Open the door and I'll tell you."

"Go away!"

"If I do," he threatened succinctly, "it will be to that nice big mansion right next door."

"That's underhanded and base!" she accused. He must know how embarrassed she'd be if Emerson confronted her "betrothed" at that hour of the morning.

"Yes, it is," he agreed loudly. "But what can I say? I'm desperate to see you! My heart never stopped pounding the whole night through!"

Now that, she thought, was an exaggeration and a half. Or was it? Memories of the night before swept over her. They had been in his bed. They'd nearly made love, and would have if she hadn't gotten panicky. Maybe it was an episode he couldn't easily forget, either.

Her skin prickled with a thousand sensations. If she let him in, she'd risk another sensual encounter. If she didn't, he'd wake up the entire neighborhood, shouting to be heard. One by one she reluctantly unfastened the locks. As the door swung open, she hung onto it defensively, resting her cheek against the edge.

Brendon grinned down at her, all easy charm. His hair was curling wildly in windblown splendor. His cheeks were tinged pink from the cold, and she saw that his jaw was freshly shaven and scented with cologne. He was dressed for work in a dark brown suit the color of his eyes, a brown-and-white pinstriped long-sleeved shirt, and a dark brown tie. His shoes were neatly polished soft leather. He held a grocery bag cradled loosely in one arm.

The reproach that had been on the tip of Savannah's tongue died at the sight of him. "Glad to see me, hm?" he asked. "You sure look nice." He leaned down to plant a soft, quick kiss on her brow. "You're warm, too."

Despite everything she was glad to see him. Don't let him walk all over you, her cautious inner voice warned. She drew back, pulled her robe tighter around her, and belted it securely. "You are without a doubt the most arrogant, presumptuous man I've ever met!"

"You're no shrinking violet yourself," he answered. He leaned closer and peered down at her, a sensual smile curving his lips.

She shot him an annoyed glance and reached for his arm. "Oh, get in here before you wake up the whole neighborhood." Her voice was still husky with sleep. "What would people think if they saw you here at this hour?"

His white teeth flashed. "Probably the worst—that I spent the night. It's a good thing we're engaged."

She shut the door and leaned against it. Very conscious of her bare toes peeking out beneath the hem of her robe, she straightened and glared peevishly at him. Abruptly his expression sobered. "We've still got a lot to talk about, Savannah," he told her gently. "We need to decide what our next move is going to be. Ending the farce may prove even more difficult and complex than beginning it was."

She ran a hand through her hair and frowned. "I guess maybe it would be better if you helped me talk to Emerson." She didn't want her grandfather to hold a grudge against Brendon for something she had dreamed up. And if she was going to try to get the two men to declare a truce, she'd have to act carefully.

Brendon shifted the grocery bag onto a nearby chair. Before she could react, he closed the distance between them and pulled her into his arms. "I admit there's another reason I came. I wanted to apologize for last night. I took advantage of you. I'm sorry. Let me make it up to you, Savannah. Please."

She thought of the understanding he'd shown when she talked about Keith. Their mock engagement aside, she did want to see him. Why deny it? Why deny herself? "How?" she asked cautiously.

He grinned. "By cooking your breakfast."

"I should throw you out on principle."

"But you won't." He grinned confidently.

No, she wouldn't. "Oh, you're impossible!" She sighed with a dramatic display of temper, but her irritation was fading fast. "I can't argue with anyone until after I've had my coffee."

"Is that a yes or a no?" he queried softly, leaning closer and running his finger across her lower lip.

How could she fight him when he pursued her at such a breathtaking rate?

"You can stay, just this once," she decided firmly. Immediately she wondered if she'd done the right thing.

"Great." He looked past her to the fireplace. "Got any wood?"

She nodded disinterestedly. "It's stored out back."

"I'll get it." Releasing her, he headed cheerily for the french doors off the kitchen. She carried the groceries in after him, then returned to the bedroom and shut the door. She ran a brush through her hair, washed her face, scrubbed her teeth, and searched through the bottom of her closet until she located some warm terry cloth slippers. She thought briefly of changing but decided against it. Let him think she wasn't the least bit unnerved by his presence. She'd just make doubly sure she kept him at arm's length. Since they were both due at their respective offices by nine o'clock, he couldn't stay long anyway.

By the time she slipped back into the living room, Brendon had returned with the wood. She watched him build a fire, admiring his ease, and then walked into the kitchen to start the coffee. He joined her moments later. His suit jacket was off, his sleeves rolled up to the elbows.

"You seem to have made yourself quite comfortable in my absence," she commented dryly. Not sure whether she should be amused or annoyed, she felt a little of both. This was her life, her home, her morning, and he'd intruded on all three yet somehow still acted as if he were doing her a favor.

"You look cozy, too. I'm glad you didn't change into anything more formal." He grinned and began removing groceries from the sack, setting eggs, bacon, croissants, and orange juice on the counter. "I think I've got everything I need." He paused as if taking inventory.

"Let's hope so," she shot back waspishly, "because if you had to go out, I'm not sure I'd let you back in again."

He laughed, soft and low. "Oh, I think I could persuade you." He shot her a raking glance.

"Don't bet on it."

His eyebrows rose at her tone, but he didn't reply. Calmly he raided her cupboards for utensils and began preparing the meal. She watched him wisk eggs in a bowl, admiring and resenting him at once. He definitely won points for persistence. Now if she could just school him in when not to show up. After a moment she laughed and murmured, "I can't believe I've got a total stranger in my kitchen cooking breakfast at six in the morning."

He poured them each a cup of coffee and handed her a mug. "After last night we're hardly strangers," he said.

She sipped the coffee, scalding her tongue. "We're supposed to be engaged. I don't even know if you've been married before."

"I haven't." He placed bacon in a pan.

"Why not?" She turned on the oven and placed the croissants in to warm.

Brendon wiped his hands on a dish towel and paused to take a sip of coffee. "First and most important, no one woman has ever really caught my eye." He glanced at her, amending, "Until now. Second"—he shrugged and turned back to the stove—"I've been very involved in building my company. That's been my chief priority."

"And are you planning to stay in Charleston, then?" she asked.

He gave her a steady look. "Oh, yes."

He seemed very sure of himself. She swallowed.

"Will *you* stay on here?" he asked her. "You said your mother was in Europe."

"Yes."

"You don't plan to join her there, not even for a vacation?"

"No. We don't get along very well." Savannah glanced down at her hands. "I've been something of a disappointment to my mother." For some reason she felt comfortable confiding in him.

"Why?" His eyes narrowed.

She grimaced. "She wanted me to be a modern-day Scarlett O'Hara, the belle of six counties. I was a serious student, very straitlaced and not all that popular. She's never forgiven me for forsaking local charity and genteel occupations for bona-fide construction, even if it is the family business."

"What about your father?" He was watching her steadily.

"My parents separated soon after I was born. Apparently Dad was too serious for Mother, too. He works for an electronics firm and lives in Japan."

"Do you ever see him?"

"Not since I was twelve."

"And I thought I had it bad," he murmured.

She took another sip of coffee, explaining matter-of-factly, "Consequently my grandfather's always been very protective of me. He used to intervene when my mother and I fought. She didn't appreciate it, and after I graduated from college, family tensions escalated. Mother wanted me to marry. So did Emerson, but he was also willing to give me a chance in the family business. Mother said no one would be interested in marrying a company executive, and she forbade Emerson to intervene. Naturally he did anyway. After some thought I decided it was time I struck out on my own, and I announced to one and all that I was going to California. Mother cried and Grandfather worried, but I went anyway." She smiled, recalling. "That was the first truly independent action I had ever taken. I was very proud of myself."

"As you should have been." With a spatula he lifted bacon strips onto paper towels.

"I did well professionally there, without any help from my grandfather or his influential friends, but I was also very lonely," Savannah admitted. "I really missed my home state."

"And that's where you married your husband?"

She nodded. "Keith was orginally from Atlanta. We came from similar backgrounds. We also shared a fondness for hominy grits, if you can believe that. Of course we could never get them anywhere in California, so we cooked them together. They never turned out right, though. They were always lumpy and tasted like paste."

She glanced up. Brendon was studying her with a dismayed expression. "What's the matter?"

"I forgot the grits."

"Ten to one you hate them." She threw back her head and laughed.

"Can't stand them," he confirmed vehemently. "And I can't tell you how many times I've ended up eating them."

"Poor baby."

He clasped his hands together theatrically and dropped to one knee. "I swear I'll never forget them again. Will you forgive me?"

"I guess I'll have to, won't I?"

He rose and stepped forward. The flirtatious exchange had sent warmth into her cheeks. As they stood for a moment, gazing at each other, Savannah forced herself to remain aloof, but she wanted to take him by the hand, lead him back to her bedroom, and curl up beside him on the sheets. She wanted to exchange life stories, talk endlessly, make love, and then make love again. A shiver passed over her at the absurdity of the fantasy and the desire it revealed. They were partners in a prank that had gone wrong, and for the moment that was all.

Brendon gently stroked the base of her throat. She knew that if he kissed her, all reason and sense of responsibility would be lost. "The eggs!" she blurted out.

Brendon turned to the stove. "You're right. They do look done."

Wordlessly she set out blue and white Currier and Ives china plates, silver, small juice glasses filled with ice, and the blue linen napkins she generally reserved for special occasions. Brendon placed the bacon, eggs, and croissants on the table. They ate silently, speaking only occasionally to ask the other to pass the butter or the crock of strawberry preserves or the wooden salt and pepper shakers. "That was delicious," she murmured at last, pushing back her plate.

Brendon slouched comfortably in his chair, a teasing glimmer in his eyes. "You know the old saying: Cook a career woman a decent meal and she'll follow you anywhere."

"Ho, ho," she said, suppressing an amused smile. She mustn't let him get too confident.

His eyes roamed her steadily, and she had the distinct impression he was trying to guess what lay beneath the snug robe. She colored slightly, thinking of the thin, sexy plum silk. "If you're awake enough now, I'd like to talk." He rose. "Perhaps the living room would be more comfortable. It will certainly be warmer."

Maybe then she could get rid of him. After adding more coffee to their mugs, Savannah followed him into the living room and sank down in one of the rose upholstered Victorian chairs. The fire was hissing softly in the grate. The morning light filtered through sheer white curtains, past the heavy velvet drapes gracing tall windows on either side of the white marbled grate. Brendon sat down on the sofa and stretched his long legs out in front of him.

"I'm still planning to speak to Emerson first thing this morning," Savannah stated plainly.

He nodded, appearing disinterested, studying a display of silk flowers. "I'm sure that would clear your conscience." He rested a shirt-covered arm across the curving back of her Victorian sofa. "I don't think it will do much for your standing in the business community, though."

A prickle of fear ran through her. Brendon knew how badly she wanted the presidency of McLean Development. He was also the one person who was in a position to prevent her from getting it, thanks to the unexpected way things had worked out the day before.

He took another sip of coffee. "In any business community there's a hierarchy of power and wealth. In Charleston it's run by a blue-blooded network of good-old-boys.

Your relationship with Emerson gives you an entree I've never had. But you also have two major considerations working against you: you're a woman, and you're divorced. In almost any other place neither would matter; your gender might even help. But here? In a business community that has traditionally been run only by men? I had a difficult enough time trying to establish myself because I was an outsider, and I wasn't trying to buck tradition by taking over what has been a male-dominated family firm. I also didn't have a recent history of personal problems and upheaval to make bankers and brokers nervous."

"What are you suggesting I do?"

"Suit yourself. But if you pull out of our mock engagement without even attempting to see it through, you'll prove to Emerson that you can't handle the high stakes of this business community. He'll know you can bid, dangerously if necessary—you more than proved that yesterday. But he'll also know that when the going gets rough, you don't have the guts to follow through."

"I resent that accusation," she shot back.

"It's true. He'll look at this engagement the same way he'd look at any business deal. The same gambling skills come into play. Face it—you've got the perfect vehicle with which to prove your ability to wheel and deal."

"I'd also be risking my personal reputation," she countered tensely, remembering Emerson's three requirements for giving her the presidency.

Brendon shrugged off her concern. "Play along with me and I promise I'll take the blame for the inevitable breakup."

Savannah studied him quietly. She could learn a lot from this powerful man. She'd be a fool not to take advantage of his hard-won knowledge of the Charleston business community. "You knew what Emerson's reaction to my ruse was going to be, didn't you?"

He ran a palm down the crease in his slacks. "I have the advantage of not being emotionally close to him. And yes, I've dealt with him enough to know how wily he can be under the most difficult circumstances. On the other hand, you're his granddaughter. You should know him better than

I do on a personal level. And you did come to me for help."

"Which I've come to regret." Her mouth twisted wryly. When would she learn to curb her impetuousness?

He grinned. "You're in up to your pretty little neck now, darling. And if you're seriously interested in obtaining that company presidency, you'd better figure out your next move."

"Obviously you have an idea."

"At the very least you should raise the stakes considerably. Emerson didn't react as you wished, but he must have been shocked to see you with me. No doubt he's aware of how late you came home last night, too. You're in a position to deal from strength this morning, Savannah. Show him you mean business. If he truly detests me as much as you seem to think, he'll back down and hand you the presidency of McLean Development without marriage in the end. In the meantime you're going to have to stick it out and prove your ability to bluff."

Savannah knew Brendon was right. She needed to prove she wasn't afraid to take a calculated risk. What she didn't trust was her ability to count on, control, or even properly read Brendon. "And you have no ulterior motive in this at all?" she questioned uneasily.

Brendon grinned and set his coffee cup aside. "The way you look right now, you can hardly blame me for wanting to continue our engagement under whatever terms. You're a beautiful and desirable woman—one I'd like very much to make love to."

Her heart hammered wildly against her ribs as he rose slowly to his feet. She stood, too, backing away in panic. "Brendon, no," she said firmly, irritated to hear a faint but unmistakable breathlessness in her voice.

He circled her indolently, crossing directly to her side only when she was backed against the front door and had placed her hand on the knob. He shook his head slowly, in silent mocking reproach. "No, sweetheart, you're not throwing me out. Not yet. Not until I've had my hello, good-bye, and in-between kisses." He lifted her wrist to his mouth and gently circled the underside with his thumb. His tongue lingered maddeningly over the erratic pulse.

She wanted to protest, pull away, stop him, but she was mesmerized by his radiant gaze. By degrees he drew her closer. Her breasts just brushed the muscular contours of his chest, and his grip was firm as his left arm circled her waist. He shifted her closer, and she trembled, her skin burning with desire. The silk gown and chenille robe provided little protection after all.

"You're not playing fair," she whispered.

"Neither are you," he asserted softly. "If you'd had any sense, you would have gotten dressed the moment I stepped through that door. All through breakfast I haven't been able to think about anything but holding you, kissing you."

His hand slid lower still and splayed intimately across her spine. Why hadn't she gotten dressed? Had she secretly wanted this to happen?

She shut her eyes slightly as she watched the slow, inevitable descent of his warm, generous mouth. He was so sexy, he made her blood boil. And he was smart, ambitious, and at least as successful as she was. He understood the business she was in, the demands it made. Sometimes she even wondered if he understood how she thought.

"We shouldn't complicate our situation," she whispered.

"Probably not," Brendon agreed. His lips traveled lightly over hers. His hands spanned her waist and slid up to her ribs. He kissed her firmly, ardently, then lightly, persuasively. "You taste so good," he whispered against her mouth. "Like coffee." He kissed her again. "And cream and strawberry jam."

She laughed huskily, despite her intention of holding him at bay. "My compliments to the chef." Her arms twined loosely around his neck, and she began to relax again, feeling less threatened.

"Thank you," he whispered back. "I'll relay the message."

Break it off now, Savannah urged herself sensibly, while you can still end it on a sweet, lazy note. But her passionate side lured her into acquiescence. She wanted to see where he would lead her.

Brendon tangled his fingers in her hair and slid his open palms across her shoulders. Her breasts throbbed with the urgent need to be touched as sensations washed over her. The crackling sounds of the fire sounded further and further away. Beyond her control, a low purr of pleasure caught deep in her throat. She felt as if she were spinning in a maelstrom of yearning. It had been so long since she had been desired, so long since she, too, had needed, wanted.

"Let me love you," he whispered. His hands edged closer to her breasts before trailing down to her waist, and he tightened his grip as his mouth touched hers lightly, then flitted away.

"Brendon..." She meant to tell him to stop, but the words wouldn't come.

"You want me." He kissed her again, more persuasively. When they could breathe again, he added, "And God knows I want you."

Her hands dropped to his shoulders, then wedged a space between them. Was this what she wanted?

"Do you want to be persuaded? Is that it?" His hands gently stroked the base of her throat.

"You're rushing me."

"Am I?"

Her breath suspended in her chest as his intent gaze sent her heart crashing against her ribs. "Decide what you want, Savannah, and then tell me. If you ask me to go, I will. If you ask me to stay..." His voice drifted off. The promise of lovemaking hung in the air.

She said nothing. She couldn't. "So the lady wants to be persuaded," he assumed softly. His mouth moved over hers more tenderly than before. His tongue swept her mouth voluptuously, only to return again and again. He nibbled the edge of her jaw, the shell of her ear. He teased her tongue with his own.

Her doubts faded with each caress. She was inundated with sensations she had never thought she would feel, suffused with the intense ardor only he had ever been able to arouse in her. With a sigh of capitulation, she moved against him and opened her lips to his ever-deepening kiss and the ardent exploration of his tongue. Desire built inside her, and she fit her torso to his hard male length. He reacted by crushing her even tighter against him. When one masculine hand slid down to untie and part her robe, she was no more capable of resisting than if she had known and loved him all her life. She wanted him. She wanted to know what it felt like to be a woman again.

Brendon eased the silk and lace-edged gown off her shoulder gently to bare one breast. When his fingers encircled her warmly, possessed her lovingly, she moaned. Her legs weakened and she arched against him, her hips tilting all too willingly against his hard thigh. "Savannah," he murmured, lifting the hem of her gown past her calves to mid-thigh. "You're a study of womanly contradictions, but oh, so compelling."

Chilly air assaulted her skin. As her bare legs brushed his trousers, reality pushed past the sybaritic wealth of sensations. What was she doing? She hardly knew this man. He didn't love her. No matter how good he made her feel or how sweetly tender he seemed, he was still a relative stranger. And she was not promiscuous. Her hand blocked his. She pushed away, breathing hard. "Brendon, don't."

"You're so beautiful," he whispered. "So soft and sweet. The way you tremble when I touch you makes my blood race. Touch me, Savannah," he implored. "Unbutton my shirt and touch me." His voice ended on a ragged note.

Desire warred with common sense. To obey would be playing with fire. Yet how many times had she imagined him bare-chested? Didn't she want to know the color and thickness of his chest hair? Didn't she want to touch him?

"Please," he whispered hoarsely. "Let me feel your soft breasts against my chest."

His steady gaze sapped the rest of her will. Slowly, with trembling fingers, she reached up to undo his tie. He watched as she struggled with the knot. The silk fell loose in a straight line on either side of his collar. Nervously, indecisively, she wet her lips, and her teeth caught on her lower lip. Their gazes locked, and she froze.

"I know this is new for you," he said softly. "I feel as

if I'm being reborn, too. Or maybe I just never knew how special love could be."

She swallowed. It had been so long since she'd been with a man, so desperately long. "I'm afraid I won't please you."

"Oh, sweetheart, you thrill me more than you know." He crushed her against him for brief ecstatic moments, then slowly released her. He was waiting. He wouldn't ask her again. She undid the button at his neck. Silently he offered her encouragement, then praise with his ardent gaze. The next button came easier. The next three were a breeze.

"Golden brown, I knew it," she murmured. In innocent delight she ran her fingers through the crisp mat of hair. His muscles rippled with tension as she explored freely. His nipples were small and brown. He groaned when she flicked them playfully with her fingernails. "Oh lord, Savannah, you're enough to drive a man insane with need."

Elation soared through her. She glowed with pride. "I never imagined it would be so exciting to arouse a man," she confessed shyly, ducking her head.

"Not just any man, I hope."

"Not just any man," she agreed.

"Good." He grinned, and his eyes raked her possessively. "Because I want you all to myself."

Her heartbeat accelerated at the confession. Gently he lowered the remaining shoulder of her gown and brushed the fabric aside, exposing her completely to his loving view. He bent to kiss her, and she welcomed the plunging heat of his tongue against hers. "Come closer," he murmured.

She stepped between his thighs, bracing her hands on his upper arms. Her breasts teased his chest hair, and his sinewy muscles contracted beneath the tips of her breasts while another cascade of pleasure soared through her. Experimentally she shifted against him, then again and again. Hot waves of passion flooded her, weakening her knees.

He murmured something against her mouth and swept her to him in a swift, rapacious movement. "You're driving me wild," he confessed. Hot, passionate kisses rained over and into her mouth. His hands slid over her waist to her hips. Then he pushed the gown past her waist. His intake of breath was sharp and immediate. She realized with a start that she was wearing no panties, not even the barest wisp of nylon. He surveyed her desirously.

Panic consumed her anew. The gown edged lower, but she resisted when his hands lightly stroked the inside of her thighs, edging closer to the velvet apex of her legs. "You're going too fast," she protested breathlessly.

"I know you're afraid. It's all right," he said soothingly between slow, tender kisses. Gently he caressed her abdomen and her satiny hips. His hands circled behind her, and he cupped her to him desirously. "I'll make it good for you, I promise."

Would he? Even so, did she dare risk the intimacy? "I . . . don't . . . want . . ." she whispered haltingly between kisses. Even to her the words sounded weak and ineffectual.

"Yes, you do," Brendon coaxed, wedging his knee firmly between hers. "We both do. If you didn't you would have kicked me out earlier. And I would have gone." Still kissing her, he slid his fingers across her stomach, down her thigh, then circled up and around. The lazy motions drove her mad. She arched impatiently against him. He touched her intimately, velvet flesh and dark curls. Unerringly he located her center, stroked, pressed, exalted. Despite her reservations and indecision, she curved against him, reveling in the warm gliding touch of his palm, delighting in his tenderness and gentle expertise. Never had lovemaking been so exquisite, so satisfying. He knew exactly how to touch her, paying homage to her as no man ever had. Pleasure consumed her, and she shook with a cataclysm of sensation. Her hands clutched his shoulders and it was all she could do to stifle a low moan.

He drew back. "Take me to your bed," he whispered. "Now."

She stared up at him through passion-dazed eyes. He waited patiently for her to make a decision. But with the cessation of his seductive moves, her sanity and common sense were returning. She scrutinized him carefully, wondering how they had progressed so swiftly to such forbidden delights. What was she doing, even contemplating a torrid, ill-advised affair?

His shirt was undone to the waist, his face flushed with desire. Despite the delay, he was every inch a hard, demanding male. Panic consumed her. The fear and doubt she'd been suppressing returned full force. Was this what she wanted? A fling with a man she wasn't even sure she could trust? A man who was her firm's arch rival?

Brendon continued to gaze down at her. The corners of his mouth dropped slightly. He brushed warm lips across her temple. She could feel the implacable imprint of his desire against her hip. "You're still having doubts, aren't you?" He sighed.

"I'm sorry." Her voice was muffled against his shirt. Confusion and disappointment made her suddenly want to cry. She bit her lower lip and blinked back hot tears of humiliation and regret.

Brendon's heart thudded against the open palms she splayed across his chest. She looked up and read frustration in his eyes. "I don't like being led on," his voice grated raggedly. "But I do understand." His mouth lifted in a weak smile. "And I guess I've had more than my hello, good-bye, and in-between kisses, at least for this morning."

She relaxed. "You're not angry?"

"I'm frustrated as hell," he ground out, walking away from her. Hands on his hips, he stared into the fire. "I knew when I started kissing you this morning that you weren't ready to make love. I hoped I could persuade you." He gave her a mischievous glance. "Serves me right, hm?"

She adjusted her gown over her shoulders and belted her robe. She flushed, not sure what to say. "Brendon, I—"

He cut her off briskly. "It's all right. I can be patient, Savannah." He gazed at her from head to toe. "And I made up my mind last night that I'll wait however long it takes."

Her pulse speeded crazily. If he touched her again, she would give in to him. "Can I get you some more coffee?" she offered inanely.

"No, I think I'd better be going." He located his jacket.

Savannah followed him to the front door and watched as he buttoned his shirt halfway up his chest.

"Thanks for breakfast," she said, opening the door, the words sounding inconsequential after all that had happened.

"My pleasure." Brendon leaned forward and placed another light, fleeting kiss on her upturned lips. His tender scrutiny kept her full attention despite the cold air assaulting them both. "Savannah, I—"

The sound of another male throat being cleared stopped him in mid-sentence and froze Savannah to the spot. She and Brendon turned simultaneously and stared into Emerson McLean's frosty blue eyes.

CHAPTER
Eight

"SAVANNAH, YOU LOOK surprised to see me," the elder gentleman said with a reproachful lift of his brows. "You shouldn't be. After all, I did promise you a ride to the office this morning," he reminded her. He paused to cast a censuring look at Brendon before continuing mildly, "We were *supposed* to discuss your—situation."

Her cheeks flamed. She was mortified by her grandfather's presence at such an inopportune moment. "I—I guess I forgot," she stammered.

"Evidently so," he agreed, still surveying her carefully. "Shall I wait while you dress or come back later after your beau has gone?"

Brendon kept his poise admirably in the wake of Emerson's thinly veiled chastisement. "Darling, maybe you should ask your grandfather to come in," he suggested pleasantly, sliding a possessive, steadying arm around her waist. "It's quite cold outside this morning."

"Please do come in." She ushered her grandfather in, appalled that she'd forgotten her manners. What was the matter with her?

"Today's weather forecast calls for a high of forty-five degrees," Brendon continued conversationally.

Emerson's gaze focused on the unfastened three buttons on his shirt and the tie loosely circling his neck. "Seems to be plenty warm in here," he commented. Brendon grinned ruefully and rubbed his jaw but did not rebutton his shirt. Savannah stared speechlessly at the floor. She'd be damned if she'd defend herself, the hour, or her choice of company. But Brendon wasn't making it easier on her, and, predictably, her grandfather was acting like a character out of a Victorian morality play.

Emerson lazily stalked the parlor, his hands folded behind his back. He stopped in front of the fireplace and warmed his hands. When he turned to face her again, his gaze dropped to the twin coffee cups on the table, then traveled to the breakfast dishes littering the kitchen. He shook his head in mute disapproval.

That did it. Whether it was his business or not, she wanted Emerson to know that Brendon had *not* spent the night. "Aren't you going to ask me what's been going on?" she asked lightly, hoping to introduce a charmingly told tale of breakfast being brought right to her door.

Emerson cut her off with a quick, indifferent wave of his hand. "Far be it from me to intrude on your personal life, Savannah. After all, I was the one who urged you to go out and"—he cleared his throat dramatically—"have a little fun. And the man *is* your fiancé. Isn't that right, Savannah?" His glare said Brendon had better be.

She swallowed. Brendon tightened his grasp and drew her reassuringly against him. "Don't worry, sir. I have no intention of leaving Savannah at the altar."

How true, she thought wryly. Particularly when he had no intention of ever meeting her there. She forced a tight smile and slipped out of his grasp. "Actually Brendon was just leaving," she informed Emerson coolly. Why didn't he button his shirt? Was he determined to embarrass her further? Didn't he understand how humiliated she felt, knowing Emerson assumed he had spent the night? Oh, fiddle dee dee, why was she so old-fashioned?

Brendon glanced at his watch. "Actually I've got a few minutes," he corrected brightly. "Can I get you a cup of coffee, Emerson? I think we've got some left. If not, I can always brew a fresh pot."

"I'd like that." Her grandfather sighed and took off his overcoat. As Brendon left the room to get the coffee, Savannah uncomfortably reviewed her options. The truth was, she had no graceful way out of such an awkward situation. Neither did it seem the appropriate time to tell Emerson that their engagement had been a hoax designed to prod him into accepting her single status. Her just-out-of-bed and thoroughly kissed look and Brendon's presence would hardly convince Emerson that she knew what she was doing and was capable of managing a safe and sane personal life, never mind a multimillion-dollar corporation.

"When you told me you were involved with Brendon Sloane, Savannah, I admit I thought it was a joke," Emerson said, sitting down in a chair next to the fireplace. His eyes met hers seriously. "I can see how wrong I was. You do care for him, don't you?" His question ended on a note of incredulity.

Savannah gulped. Until three days ago she hadn't even wanted to date. How could she explain all that had happened now, especially when she could barely understand it herself? "He's just so different from anyone I've ever known," she offered, folding her hands together and perching on the edge of the sofa.

Brendon strolled back in, silver serving tray in hand. He stooped before Emerson and waited while the older man took the appointed cup. She was relieved to see that Brendon had at last rebuttoned his shirt and neatly knotted his tie. "Savannah's one in a million," he said sincerely.

Emerson shook his head as he studied them both. "And I thought I was too old to be surprised."

Brendon sat down on the sofa, scooting uncomfortably close to her. One large hand settled firmly between her knee and mid-thigh. He patted her affectionately before returning his hand to his lap. Suddenly it was all she could do not to retrieve her cup of cold coffee and slosh it into his face. Why did he insist on overplaying his hand! And why, oh why had she ever enlisted this rakehell's assistance?

Silence filled the room. The two men exchanged wary glances. Savannah was glad dueling was out of fashion. She lowered her eyes. Her grandfather had asked her to present a stable personal and professional image, and only one day later she'd already put a sizable dent in her reputation. Maybe the best strategy was simply to go to work and forget the whole ridiculous situation, at least for a few hours.

"Good heavens, look at the time." She stood up abruptly. "If I don't hurry I'll be late for my meeting with John Crawford. If you men will excuse me..." She glanced pointedly at the front door.

Her less-than-tactful suggestion that both men leave failed completely. Brendon tossed her a smile and stretched his arm across the back of the sofa, and Emerson sipped his coffee delicately and stared at the floral pattern of the rug. "I'll entertain your grandfather," Brendon offered graciously. "Don't worry about a thing."

That was like asking the poor to disregard inflation! Honestly, she thought, Brendon didn't have to look quite so at home. His presence there at such an ungodly hour was more than injurious. "How thoughtful," she said sweetly, "but shouldn't you be at the office, darling? I'm sure my grandfather won't mind waiting for me alone. He can read the morning paper."

"Nonsense, my work can wait," Brendon countered equably, picking a piece of lint off his trousers. Her tight grin masked her gritted teeth. With Emerson observing her carefully, there was nothing to do but leave gracefully. She could deal with Brendon later. "As you wish. If you gentlemen will excuse me, I'll get ready for work."

And figure out what to do next, she added silently. Brendon seemed determined to thwart her efforts to tell Emerson the truth. Considering what had just happened, he was probably right; the time for truth telling had passed. But when would it get easier? The longer the ruse continued, the more difficult it would be to explain. And wasn't she proving herself unstable and indecisive by letting Brendon call the shots? True, he did seem to have more poise than she did in certain situations, but he wasn't so closely connected to Emerson, either. Should she just sit back and let him maneuver them out of the fiasco, as he had promised he eventually would?

When she emerged from the bedroom half an hour later, Emerson and Brendon were standing side by side at her kitchen sink washing dishes. "I made your grandfather some breakfast," Brendon remarked casually, handing Emerson the last glass to dry.

She stared at them incredulously. To her knowledge, Emerson had never cleared a table in his life, never mind dried a dish. "I'm glad the two of you are getting along so well." Did she sense a new camaraderie between the two rivals? Or were they just making the best of an awkward situation for her sake? "Ready to go?" she asked her grandfather.

He and Brendon exchanged glances. Brendon said, "I offered to drive you to the office, darling."

"And since I'm running terribly late, I agreed." Emerson retrieved his suit jacket and overcoat. "I need to stop at the bank first."

The last thing she needed was to spend more time alone with Brendon. "Why don't we all take our own cars?" she suggested. "Then no one will be at the mercy of anyone else's schedule."

"You two work it out." Emerson lifted his hands in a quick good-bye as he strode to the door. "See you at the office later, sweetheart," he promised. "I've got to dash."

She waited until they were alone then faced Brendon cantankerously. "You realize, don't you, that my grandfather is now truly convinced we're madly in love?"

Brendon shrugged into his jacket and straightened his tie. His smile was both blissful and mocking. "Aren't we?"

"No!" The denial emerged more vehemently than she'd intended, and she turned away, her mouth twisting in a grimace of annoyance. Damn the man! He had a habit of making her lose her composure. "But as long as we're discussing our grievances—"

"Were we?"

"We're about to!" she said shortly. "Why in heaven's name didn't you get out when I gave you the signal?" she demanded impatiently.

"Because I thought it would be more fun to stay."

"You do have an ingratiating way of making yourself right at home!" she stormed. Illogical and unreasonable as it was, she blamed him for the whole quandary. Certainly she could have bailed out at any time previously if he hadn't been so intent on keeping them "engaged."

"I don't know why you're complaining," he countered with an innocent shrug. "Emerson liked my cooking. And we did clean up the kitchen."

"That's not what I meant and you know it! The next time it happens—if it happens again, and I doubt it—I want you to leave." She'd never again open the door for him at dawn, no matter how loud he pounded.

"Are you upset because Emerson caught you in a faintly compromising situation or because he interrupted our goodbye?"

She flushed at his faintly mocking expression and refused to dignify his question with an answer. "The least you could have done when he came in was button your shirt!"

"I did, at the first unobtrusive opportunity," he corrected calmly. "As for leaving, I wasn't going to dash off in a blind panic just because Emerson appeared. You were looking guilty and embarrassed enough for the both of us. We *weren't* doing anything wrong, Savannah."

She blushed fiercely, despite her efforts not to. "Maybe not, but—"

"I want to be with you, and you want to be with me. At least you did this morning," he said softly, stepping closer. "What's wrong with that?"

"Nothing." She swallowed, trying to be unaffected. But the moment his hand touched her arm, her heartbeat raced. Blood roared in her ears, deafening her to everything else.

"You were the one still in your robe," Brendon pointed out.

He didn't have to remind her of that mistake, she thought crossly. She'd already berated herself a thousand times. "That," she said imperiously, "was meant as a power play. I didn't want you to think I'd be uncomfortable no matter how I was dressed," she confessed archly, embarrassed. "It's not as if I were a twenty-year-old virgin."

"Oh, but you are in so many ways," Brendon murmured, lifting her chin gently. He surveyed her with a tenderness that made her throat tighten. "And I'd like to be the one to reverse that shyness," he said softly.

"Stop changing the subject." She'd meant the words to be harsh and reproachful. Oddly, they sounded more like a caress.

"Have lunch with me," he suggested.

"I can't." She turned away and broke free of his light grasp. She couldn't think clearly when he held her that way, gazing down at her so intently.

He didn't try to persuade her. Aware of his eyes burning into her, she walked briskly to the closet and pulled out her winter coat. He crossed swiftly to her side and held it word-lessly for her.

"You're not upset that Emerson found us together, are you?" she asked. His composure contrasted with her lin-gering discomfiture. Was it possible he had planned it? He'd been there the previous afternoon when Emerson had offered to come by and drive her to work.

"It's not as if Emerson interrupted anything," Brendon said casually. His scrutiny made her flush. She had almost made love with him. She could still recall with breath-robbing intensity what it felt like to have his hands softly caressing and molding her flesh. She knew how crisp his chest hair was, the exact shade of it, how it looked in the morning light. Would he carry similar images around with him, images of her?

To cover her confusion she said, "You knew my grand-father was supposed to drive me to work, didn't you? That's why you were here."

"I never meant to compromise you," he said solemnly.

"As for Emerson dropping by, I forgot." He gave her a level look. "I assume you did, too. If I had remembered, I assure you I'd have been long gone before he arrived."

She stared at the floor in confusion. Was he telling the truth?

He stepped closer, his hands circling her back and sliding lightly up and down her spine until shivers engulfed her from head to toe. "On a practical level, my presence here did convince Emerson we were seriously involved," he said. "For the moment we hold the high card. Stay cool, stay in the game, and you may get that company presidency yet— even without marrying me."

Brendon walked her to her car and made sure she was safely buckled in. "I'll check with you later about lunch," he said insistently, leaning forward to brush her temple with his lips. She opened her mouth to protest, but he closed the car door, cutting off her reply.

She watched him as he strode away, reluctantly admiring his long gait. The man was devastatingly attractive—and as gentle as he was hell raising. The combination both intrigued and frightened her. She knew a close relationship with him would not be easy, but it would be exciting and pleasurable. After an unhappy marriage, an emotionally wrenching divorce, and a year alone, that prospect in itself was enough to tempt her beyond common sense. And that was what worried her. She was ripe for a love affair, and Brendon knew it.

As she drove to work she thought back over the events of the morning. Although her grandfather had been dismayed to find Brendon in her carriage house shortly after dawn, he'd been gracious about it in the end. Brendon had prepared breakfast for the man who had forced his company to lose the multimillion-dollar Edisto Island—now Paradise—land deal. What was really going on between them? Why did she feel as if she was somehow unwittingly at the crux of their truce?

John Crawford was waiting for her when she arrived at her office. He ran a hand across his balding head and slumped wearily into a chair next to her desk. "Emerson gave me the rough draft of your plans for the Edisto Island condominium project," he began.

"Paradise," she corrected. The sooner the entire staff began referring to it by its new name, the better.

"I have no quarrel with your ideas. The implementation of them, however, might be a bit difficult. You're aware, of course, of how hard it will be to construct the clubhouse restaurant and bar, as well as the mini shopping plaza of seven boutiques, and still make our proposed opening date? The golf course and tennis courts we can handle."

"I've yet to get the complete estimates from accounting and the architectural department, but yes, I do know what McLean Development is going to undertake. So does Emerson. He's given his complete approval. All that remains is the presentation to the board and the appointing of a subcontractor to help us out."

"Which brings us to problem number two," Crawford pronounced. "Sloane Construction is the only firm in the area with a crew large enough to handle such a big addition to the resort on such short notice."

"I see no problem with hiring them if no one else is available, but I have yet to be fully convinced that that is indeed the case," she said carefully.

"There's no way on earth Emerson is going to approve of hiring Sloane, not after the ruckus Sloane raised when he lost the initial Edisto Island—Paradise—bid."

She considered what Brendon had confided. If he'd lost the deal because of collusion on the part of the old-boy network—and she assumed he had—Brendon had had a right to be upset. "Why did he lose that deal, John?" she asked casually, pretending to sort through her mail. "Didn't he do all the legwork on it, talk to the owners, and arrange the sale?"

John nodded. "The local bank said he was financially overextended. And at that time interest rates were still on the way up. They had to go with someone with a better line of credit."

"Which meant our firm."

"We've been around for almost fifty years, as opposed to Sloane's five," John elaborated. "And our company does business in a more conservative manner. At least we did," he added, scowling down at her new plans for Paradise.

"Look, John, if any other firm is available, I'll do my best to hire them. The most important thing is to finish the Paradise project according to my new specifications before the April first opening date. I admit that's going to be a gargantuan project. Beyond that we've also got to refine the marketing approach so that the villas will sell."

Crawford sighed, still looking worried. "Well, lord knows I've got enough to do riding herd on the sales staff, managers, and bankers, not to mention accounting and architecture. Emerson's been less able to direct us, too."

"Precisely why he's retiring," she said. "And I'm stepping in to help out. I've got a financial stake in this firm, too, John."

"I sure hope you know what you're committing yourself to," he said finally, propelling his rotund frame from the chair. "Because McLean Development is investing a lot more capital in Paradise than we'd planned. And if those seaside condos don't sell, we're going to be stuck with one hell of a liability."

She had studied the market extensively—the buying trends, slumps, and pinnacles of the past ten years. She knew what was motivating the current breadwinners and other people in their late twenties and early thirties—the prime home buying years—to purchase real estate. The problem was convincing the sales staff that she was right in her projections and seeing their enthusiasm for success spill over to the customers. "The villas will sell, John. Take my word for it."

"Success in regard to Paradise will certainly earn you the respect of everyone employed by this firm." He relaxed slightly. As he departed he cautioned, "Just don't forget you'll be watched by the whole business community. Personal stability is what you have to prove, Savannah. A low-key, respectable private and professional life are what you need to move up in this city and in this firm."

CHAPTER
Nine

SAVANNAH WAS STILL knee-deep in new sales presentations for Paradise when Brendon entered her office shortly before noon. He lounged against the door frame, his eyes sparkling, his face lit by a cheerful grin. "Ready for lunch, sweetheart?"

He seemed prepared for another erotic encounter. Their mock engagement was fast becoming more than a joke. Her attraction for him was real and potent, but the more involved she let herself become, the more hurt she would suffer later. Hedging, she gestured at the paperwork inundating her desk. "I'm sorry, I thought I made it clear this morning that I can't go. I'm getting ready for a special session with the sales force next week. I want to give them a preview of what to expect after the board gives their approval."

"Confident, aren't you." Brendon straightened indolently from the wall.

She met his level look with a regal toss of her head. "I have every reason to be."

He came closer, glancing briefly at the papers. "Paradise?"

"None other." She knew by the way he was looking at her that he hadn't accepted her excuse about lunch. By the time he reached her desk, her heart seemed to be pounding in her throat, but she schooled herself to show no visible reaction to his presence.

"I want you with me at lunch this afternoon, Savannah." Gently capturing her hands, he lifted her implacably from her chair.

A masculine throat cleared behind them. Brendon and Savannah turned toward the sound. Her grandfather stood in the doorway, an oddly pleased expression on his face. "Sloane's right, you know." Emerson sighed. "You should take more time off, Savannah. Besides that, the two of you have an important errand to do."

"Oh?" Her eyebrows lifted. Brendon grinned.

Emerson shrugged. "You don't have an engagement ring yet, Savannah, and you really should have one before the party."

"What party?" She turned to Brendon. "What's he talking about?"

"I expect he means the engagement party he's planning to throw." Brendon kept a firm grip on her hands.

"Engagement party!" Was this another joke? Why wouldn't Brendon let go of her? "Did you know about this, darling?" she asked him with mock sweetness.

"Emerson and I discussed it briefly this morning." He returned her smile lovingly.

"And didn't tell me?" It was difficult to keep the outrage from her voice.

"Your grandfather thought it would be a nice surprise," Brendon explained.

"We're going to hold it at the Rolling Hills Country Club. I've had three secretaries phoning out invitations all morning." Emerson beamed.

"How thoughtful," she replied politely, though she felt

as if a thousand butterflies were doing a tap dance in her stomach. "When's the party?" Maybe she could feign a good case of malaria.

"Tonight," Emerson explained. Her heart sank as he pulled a note pad from his pocket and checked his calendar. "Sloane and I both thought it would be a good idea to go public with the announcement as soon as possible. I understand from the secretary that there have already been some rumors about you. Apparently I wasn't the only one who saw your Mercedes parked in front of the carriage house, son." Emerson pinned Brendon with a steady, reproachful gaze and cleared his throat.

Brendon's mouth curved slightly. "We'll do our best to be more discreet, sir," he promised dryly.

Emerson held up both palms and, before Savannah could explain, said, "I know how it is to be young and in love. Seeing you married, Savannah, is the best retirement present I could have. Frankly, John Crawford and I have talked extensively about this. More and more he's resisting the demands the presidency would put on his personal life. But with you happily settled here in Charleston, and having successfully opened the Paradise project, you'll be able to assume the presidency under the best possible terms."

Savannah imagined what Emerson had described: she and Brendon married, presiding over rival construction firms. What would happen when the first sought-after property was up for bids? "I've been thinking," she said, breaking free of Brendon's possessive grasp. "What about the question of conflict of interest? My being married to Brendon and also being president of McLean Development is bound to cause problems." Maybe this was her way out. Maybe she wouldn't have to reveal her impetuous scam after all. Heaven knew she'd never repeat anything like it again.

But Brendon cut in just as smoothly. "Naturally Emerson and I discussed that problem at length this morning."

"Which is another reason we're having this party tonight," Emerson added. "To show our friends and business associates that although the two of you may be engaged, your private lives will have no bearing on your professional interests—except perhaps to make our business dealings run a little more smoothly. Certainly neither firm will be expected to give unnecessary quarter to the other simply because you're engaged."

Or in other words, she thought wryly, the rivalry could continue full blast once the social amenities were taken care of and stockholders and board members had been mollified. "Why do I feel as if I've been caught between a rock and a hard place with nowhere to go but down?" she joked weakly.

"Perhaps because you have been by your unexpected choice of beau," Emerson countered. "However, the course of true love never did run smooth." He seemed to be waiting for her to give in. She thought of the company presidency and how much she still wanted it.

"Don't worry, darling," Brendon said soothingly. "I'm sure there isn't anything you can't handle once you put your mind to it, including the presidency of McLean Development and being engaged to me."

Emerson left shortly for a business meeting. Savannah watched him disappear down the carpeted hallway and turned back to the stacks of proposals littering her desk. Hands on his hips, Brendon watched as she reached for a pen. "What are you doing?" she asked a moment later when she realized that despite the fact that she was ignoring him, he still refused to leave.

"Waiting for you. We have a luncheon appointment, in case you've forgotten."

Her jaw tightened truculently. "I told you I'm not going."

"I'm staying right here until you're ready."

With an oath she went back to her papers. Five minutes later she realized she hadn't understood a word she'd read. She considered calling security and having Brendon tossed out, but realizing how much additional gossip such an action would prompt, she decided against it.

She tossed down her pen and turned to him. Brendon was perusing the papers on her desk over her shoulder. She flipped them over determinedly, irritated because she hadn't noticed before that he'd been reading. "How am I going to get you out of my life?"

"Marry me." He stepped closer, his nearness affecting her like a caress.

She fought a shiver by crossing her arms beneath her breasts. "That's not funny."

He sighed. "Neither is this engagement party your grandfather's planning to give."

She could read no expression in his face except slight annoyance. "Why didn't you back out of it—or give me fair warning?"

He shook his head. "Because I wasn't sure he was serious when he mentioned it this morning. He seemed to be waiting for me to object. When I didn't, he said something vague about doing it right away. I didn't realize he meant this evening until he called my secretary at about nine-thirty and asked for a list of guests I'd like to have receive phoned invitations. I didn't tell you earlier because I knew it would upset you and you wouldn't get any work done. Besides, we had a date for lunch. I figured I'd break it to you then in person."

His explanation made sense. She stared at him warily, then said, "But we didn't have a lunch date. I never said I'd go."

"You didn't say you wouldn't, either."

"Only because you shut the door before I could respond."

"You could have rolled down the car window and shouted your refusal."

He had a point. She hadn't really wanted to object that vehemently.

"Besides, we still have to buy the ring."

She rose from her chair and stalked over to the window. "Don't you think this joke has gone far enough?"

"For the sake of your reputation, we have to go through with it now," he said gently. "I'm sorry about my car being in front of your carriage house this morning. I didn't think. Sometimes I forget Charleston is such a small town."

"You could have stayed away."

"It would have been smarter," he agreed, "but I didn't."

His calm acceptance infuriated her. "The least you could have done was park half a block away," she accused with bad temper. By starting a fight and staying angry and defensive, maybe she could keep her growing attraction under control.

"And make it look as if we really had something to hide?" he queried, arching his brow.

She fell silent, thinking of everything that had happened. He'd been tender, understanding, kind, and sexy, as well as high-handed and arrogant. If their liaison were not hindered by the complications of the prank, she would have moved heaven and earth to be with him. "Would you really go through with this engagement party just to protect my reputation?" she asked.

He looked solemnly down at her. "I never meant to hurt you," he said quietly, "even when I was angry with you for trying to use me to get to Emerson. Now that I'm getting to know you, I find myself wanting to protect you all the time. And that's the truth." He straightened, checking his watch. "We'd better leave if we want to get a ring before the party tonight."

She surveyed him hesitantly. He made her feel so vulnerable. But he did seem to have her best interests at heart. "I guess we have to think of your reputation, too." She sighed at last. After all, she had dragged him into the practical joke, not the other way around. "We'll buy the ring. But then, Brendon, we really have to plan a way out of this mess!"

He strolled with her to the parking lot behind the McLean Development building and got into his Mercedes.

"Why don't we have a big quarrel right after Paradise has officially opened?" he suggested. "Surely you'll have proved yourself professionally capable by then. And with Emerson's retirement only a month away and Crawford no doubt still resisting the presidency, I'll wager Emerson will hand you the position regardless." Brendon spoke as he directed the car through Charleston's winding city streets, gazing straight ahead as he maneuvered through the stop-and-start motions of traffic. "Until then we can play it by ear, take it one step at a time."

They didn't seem to have a choice. Because so many of the guests had already been notified, Savannah couldn't back out of the party without embarrassing her grandfather and looking irresponsible.

Brendon parked in front of a jewelry store on Meeting Street. His arm circled her shoulders, and, oblivious to the noon hour congestion on the sidewalks, he slid closer. His free hand stroked her cheek. "I missed you this morning," he confided. "You're all I've been able to think about. Tell me you missed me, too."

Her throat felt unaccountably dry. "I . . ."

"Tell me." He drew her even closer into his heated embrace.

"I thought about you all morning," she replied in a reluctant, throaty murmur. Did he need to hear her say that because of ego? Or was he feeling as enamored as she was? Her heart soared with the possibility. Was he beginning to care for her?

His palm pressed against her waist and slid underneath her blue wool suit jacket to her white silk blouse. He kneaded her spine with a sensual expertise that made her arch hungrily toward him. A low gasp escaped her parted lips, and she buried her face in his hard shoulder. "We shouldn't—" she began to protest, but the people on the sidewalk seemed further and further away. The world was narrowing. The sounds of their breathing made a ragged, alluring background against which to make love.

Brendon's arm tightened. He sighed. "I keep telling myself I'm a fool to get so involved with you, but I can't seem to help it any more than I can help kissing you now."

His mouth moved hungrily over hers as his free hand wove in her hair, framed her face, cupped her chin. Fire sped along her nerve endings; her bones melted beneath the passionate intensity of his kiss. She wound her arms around his neck and shifted desirously close. The last of her reserve fled as she met him kiss for passionate kiss, stroking the edges of his teeth with her tongue, tasting, exploring, learning anew the warm, moist cavern of his mouth. She had never known such perfection. She had never been forced to exercise such restraint.

Brendon was breathing rapidly when he pulled back slightly. He studied her tenderly and admitted, "I wish you'd never come to me with that crazy request. It would make the situation so much simpler if we weren't engaged, weren't officers of rival companies. I want you, Savannah," he admitted harshly, "more desperately than I've ever wanted a woman."

She couldn't form a reply. If she said she desired him, he'd take her to bed. She couldn't chance making love with him, knowing she was falling in love with him. It would hurt too much when the affair ended; and it would end, she reminded herself sternly. Hadn't he been making plans just minutes before to end their engagement with a well-timed quarrel?

He scrutinized her steadily. His index finger outlined her trembling lips and slipped between them to part her teeth. She felt an answering flutter in her abdomen as his head slanted slowly toward her. She was aware of the slight smokiness of their breath in the cooling car and the scent of his aftershave. His mouth fit against hers, as gently tender as his initial possession had been passionate. Like velvet, his tongue outlined her lips and moved between them. She tasted the sweetness that was uniquely his, then gave herself up to the delightful pressure of his tongue, to the way his body shifted closer, to the warmth she drew from his embrace. Flames of desire licked at her veins as his hands slid down her arms to her shoulders and around her back.

A horn blaring and the voices of curious people on the sidewalk reminded her where they were. He had done it again, she thought as he released her at last. She frowned, feeling dizzy and disoriented. He had made her forget everything but his touch, that moment, and the special ardor generated between them. Was this love? Or was it pure, unadulterated physical need? No one else had ever made her feel so cherished.

Brendon assisted her from the car. With the winter sun shining brightly, it was a beautiful though briskly chilly day. With his arm around her waist, Brendon directed her toward the jewelry store. "Think of this as a dress rehearsal for this evening," he instructed imperiously. "I want you to give every appearance of being madly in love with me."

He spoke like a teacher grimly instructing a dull student. She dug in her heels. Was that what the passionate interlude in the car had been about? A practice session for the evening's formalities? How cold-blooded could he be?

He glanced at her with exasperation. "I don't have time to argue with you. Just do as I say!"

How dare he order her around? "What are you going to do if I don't?" she shot back in a vehement whisper. "Drag me around by the hair, cave-man style?"

His arm still around her waist, he directed her out of the path of pedestrians toward the windows of the jewelry store. Suddenly she knew she couldn't go through with the engagement, no matter what was at stake. It was too dishonest.

"I've changed my mind," she said haughtily, slipping free of his grasp. "I don't want a ring after all." And she didn't want him as her beau!

But before she could escape, his hands shot out on either side of her, trapping her against the glass. "We can't have an engagment party without a ring," he said quietly. She glared mutinously at him. His jaw tightened, and a muscle worked convulsively in his cheek.

"Fine." She slid beneath his outstretched arm. "Then buy it and wear it yourself!"

She got approximately two steps before he clamped a hand on her shoulder. Before she could utter a gasp of protest, he swung her around to face him. She bumped into his chest, her head tilted back. "We're going into that store and buy a ring now," he said fiercely through gritted teeth, tightening his grip. "And so help me, you'd better behave!"

Several people stepped around them. Shoppers glanced at them, amused. Savannah's resentment flared higher. "As you wish," she said with sweet sarcasm.

His gaze narrowed suspiciously, but he released her.

Together they walked to the store entrance. If he wanted to go inside, they would, but that didn't mean they'd find anything that would live up to her specifications!

Brendon led her to a clerk. "I'd like to buy an engagement ring for my fiancée," he said quietly.

She walked forward and interrupted. "And I know exactly what I want!" She was aware of Brendon tensing behind her, and satisfaction made her smile. She strolled over to the display case and gazed greedily down. "I want a diamond, a big garnet, and three sapphires all in one setting." She flashed Brendon a mock-adoring grin.

He laughed uneasily. "She's kidding."

"No, I'm not." She looked innocently at the clerk.

Brendon placed both hands on her shoulders and turned her toward him. He leaned closer and spoke with exaggerated patience. "Sweetheart, wouldn't you prefer a single diamond in one setting? I'll get you a big one, I promise."

The jeweler puffed out his chest and added in a helpful tone, "A classic selection, sir. It's so traditional."

"It's dull," she retorted plaintively, "and the answer is no. I want something that really sparkles."

Brendon spoke again in a strained voice. "Let's put it this way, darling. A single stone is all I can afford."

She was aware of the assets of his company and knew that wasn't true. "Can't you put it on time payments?" she suggested.

He grimaced. "I don't think we want to pay the interest."

"Actually . . ." The jeweler cleared his throat helpfully.

"One stone," Brendon decided flatly. "And that's it."

"That's final?" Adopting the tone and manner of a petulant child, she steadfastly ignored the anger in his eyes. "Yes."

"Oh, well." Savannah waved her hand airily and shrugged. "In that case, I won't take anything." With an apologetic glance at the jeweler, she headed toward the exit. "Sorry we wasted your time."

"Stay where you are," Brendon commanded to the salesman. He caught her arm and pulled her in a wide circle. She stood in front of him, her face tilted up to his. "You know as well as I do that this is one chore that has to be done right now, regardless," he pointed out calmly. "And I think we've wasted enough of the salesman's time."

She pitied the man, but not enough to cooperate with Brendon. "If I can't have the garnet along with the sapphires and the diamond . . ." she began. She knew she was pushing Brendon past his limit, but she didn't care.

"We'll take a diamond. The largest stone you have will be fine," Brendon informed the clerk over her head.

The jeweler gave a sigh of relief. "Platinum gold or yellow?"

Savannah's frustrations made her reckless and disruptive. "Zinc," she demanded.

"Platinum," Brendon contradicted. "We'll need the engagement ring sized right away."

"Yes, sir." The salesman practically saluted in his glee as he tallied up the bill.

"Still want to marry me?" Savannah asked angrily.

"More than ever." There was a finality in Brendon's voice that chilled her to the bone.

When their business was finished a few minutes later, they left the store, a huge diamond ring glittering on Savannah's finger. "I never thought I'd say this," Brendon muttered, "but I think I need a drink."

"Suit yourself. I want to go back to the office—now," Savannah stated. His footsteps echoed behind her on the cement, but she refused to face him. If he was half as upset as she was they might start an entirely new McLean-Sloane feud, one that would be even more difficult to resolve.

His steps overtook hers with a lazy indolence she found extremely annoying. He stepped in front of her, blocking her way to his car. "You promised you'd eat lunch with me. I'm holding you to that."

"Oh, really?"

"Yes, really."

When she moved as if to continue down the sidewalk, he blocked her path again. A sigh of exasperation whistled softly through her teeth. He faced her passively, his gaze icy. Fury engulfed her anew. "Go to—"

He caught her against him in one swift motion. His hands pinioned her arms to her sides. "Don't push me, Savannah," he ground out between clenched teeth. "I've had all I can take this morning—first from Emerson and now from you. Now what's it going to be? Do you want to hash this problem out over a nice quiet lunch and a drink, or do you want to have it out right here?" He leaned over her, his face etched in taut, uncompromising planes.

Now that he mentioned it, she was hungry. "You're paying?"

He released his grip and rolled his eyes. "Yes."

"Good. I'm going to order the most expensive item on the menu."

He laughed, and the fight left her as swiftly as it had come. Suddenly she, too, was exhausted. It had been a depleting day, the previous afternoon had not been any easier, and they still had an engagement party to suffer through later that evening. She had to admit he'd been a fairly good sport. "I'm sorry I've behaved so childishly," she said.

"I need to be alone with you, Savannah," he confessed softly. He took her cool hand and rubbed it between his warm ones. "I need a few minutes without the crazy complications of our engagement."

She nodded. The silence stretched comfortably between them as they returned to his car and drove the three blocks to the restaurant he'd selected. As soon as they were seated, Brendon ordered a bottle of wine, and although it was unusual for her to drink during the noon hour of a working day, Savannah sipped the Chablis gratefully. She needed the break. She needed time to think.

Unfortunately, even when the conversation turned to fanciful matters, the diamond she wore reminded her of the chaos in their lives. It flashed brilliantly whenever it caught the dimmest light, drawing her unwilling attention. "I can't get used to anything this heavy," she said, removing the beautiful ring and setting it beside her plate.

"You don't like it?" Brendon picked it up and studied her face.

"We could always go back and let you pick out something else," he offered.

The truth was, it made her feel as if she really were engaged. She shook her head. "No. It was far too expensive as it was. I'll reimburse you." She frowned. "I suppose I could try to return it later."

"Keep it. I'll pay for it," he offered succinctly.

She glanced at him in astonishment. "Don't be ridiculous!"

He surveyed her with studied detachment. Apparently not liking what he saw, he glanced around the room with disinterest, his gaze lingering on the potted plants that stood against the papered and wainscotted walls. "Believe me"— he grinned, finishing the last of his coffee—"you're going to earn every penny."

She froze. Here was the cold-hearted businessman she was beginning to fear. Her spine stiffened; her breath seemed lodged in her throat. "What do you mean?"

"Emerson's initial assessment of me was right," Brendon told her. "I am a clever rascal. And I don't go to this much trouble to help a lady in distress unless there's something in it for me. And up until now you've been decidedly unenthusiastic about this scam. Your lukewarm performance wouldn't fool anyone."

"But we're not in love!"

"Speak for yourself, sweetheart." Deliberately Brendon slipped the diamond ring back onto her finger. "You may whiz in and out of poker games at will, but I don't. Once I'm in, I'm in until the very end."

"If I want to quit, Brendon, I will." She refused to let him intimidate her. "You can't force me to continue playing a part!"

He shrugged. "Your grandfather already has doubts about your surviving in the wheeling and dealing business world." He glanced at her unfinished meal. "Fold and you'll prove he's right."

Her appetite for rich stuffed mackerel faded completely. She watched as Brendon added another packet of sugar to a fresh cup of coffee and swirled it around with a spoon.

"What do you want from me?" she demanded, unable to decide whether to glare or give in.

"What I indicated last night." He reached across the table and captured her trembling hand with his own. He stroked her wrist with soothing motions. But the pragmatic tone of his next words cut off whatever ardor she might have felt. "I want the contracts to the additional building going on at Paradise. Consider it a way of evening the score for McLean Development having cheated my firm out of the property in the first place. Consider it anything you like"—his voice lowered warningly—"as long as I get the results before the end of the week."

Inside she was panicking, but she kept a composed demeanor. "We're doing more building than we initially planned. We haven't asked for outside bids or subcontractors."

He laughed mirthlessly. "Don't play coy with me, Savannah. I know it's just a matter of time. I've got a friend over in the zoning commission at Edisto Island. I know exactly how much additional building you have planned for Paradise. I also know McLean Development doesn't begin to have the resources to complete the new plans and still make the proposed April first launch date. Without the amenities such as the on-site restaurant, bar, and mini shopping mall, you and I both know those condominiums won't sell worth a plugged nickel—not in today's buyer's market, even with the prime oceanfront location.

"And if you delegate all the building to McLean, you'll never make your launch date. Without that you might as well forget the whole project for another year, because you won't sell oceanfront villas in the winter—not in Carolina. And not to sell for a year would leave McLean Development with an awful lot of debt and no capital to invest elsewhere. So you see, Savannah, you really have no choice. You have to build as proposed, and you need help to do it. I'm offering to supply the subcontracting at reasonable rates. The work will be top quality."

"That's all very nice, but the decision has not been made yet."

"You've got control of the project," he pointed out complacently. "Stop looking around for another firm or firms and award the extra contracting to Sloane Construction. My crews could start this week."

He built a convincing argument, but she didn't like being pushed into anything. She liked even less his high-handed attempts at persuasion. "What happens if I award it to another firm?"

He released his grip on her hand and sat back against the booth. "I go to the local home builders' association with inside information on how you do business. I tell them about your attempts to use me to gain control of your grandfather's firm."

"But that was a joke!" she burst out impatiently. "At least until you jumped in and announced our plans to marry!"

"You didn't deny it at the time," he shot back coolly.

"How could I have trusted you?" She tossed her napkin onto her plate. "You're despicable—as low as my grandfather said!"

His hand covered her wrist, and a muscle worked convulsively in his cheek. "I'm also ambitious," he reminded her flatly. "My firm needs that work. And like it or not, you—the next president of McLean Development—may just have provided me with the key to getting it."

"After what you've done today?" she shot back reaching for her purse and rising. "I wouldn't employ your firm to lay so much as a simple sidewalk!"

He stood, dropped two bills on the table, and followed her lazily to the door. Before she could hail a cab, he had captured her elbow in an unbreakable grip. "I'll drive you back to the office," he said in a soft voice.

Because there were other people within earshot, she did not resist. They walked silently to his car. He held her door, but she refused to look at him or acknowledge his presence in any way.

He waited until he had parked in front of McLean Development's downtown office before speaking again. "I'll pick you up around eight."

Insults and denials crowded her mind. Then she thought

of her grandfather and the trouble he had gone to arranging the impromptu party. "It will be our last date, Mr. Sloane," she said icily, getting out of the car. She heard his low, soft laugh follow her as she stormed up the walk, and she cursed him with every step.

CHAPTER
Ten

SAVANNAH'S DOORBELL RANG at precisely eight o'clock. "Change your mind about going through with this?" she asked hopefully as she ushered Brendon inside. Her heart pounded at his proximity. Unwillingly she took in the silk-blend tuxedo, the black making a striking contrast against his pleated white shirt.

"Not a chance, sweetheart." His eyes met hers steadily.

She struggled to ignore his sensual presence. She would tell Emerson tomorrow, she decided. Together the two McLeans would devise a graceful way out of the engagement.

"Ready to go?" Brendon waited restlessly.

"I'll get my wrap." She reached for the glittery black evening stole on the chair next to the door. Chivalrously he slipped it over her shoulders. He frowned, glancing at her dress. She'd selected a snug-fitting gold-threaded black eve-

118

ning gown. Long sleeved, the gown bared one arm and shoulder in a seductive swath from her collarbone to low across her breast.

"You're wearing black to an engagement party?" He sounded surprised.

"Consider my mourning our own private joke." She led the way to the car.

The party was already in full swing by the time they arrived. They spent the first hour greeting guests who had flown or driven in from all over the state. "This place sounds like a *Who's Who* of Southern businessmen," she murmured when she'd slipped away for a small glass of the nonalcoholic punch.

Brendon sipped champagne. "Knowing Emerson and the fact that you're his only heir and the beneficiary of McLean Development, I wouldn't have expected anything less."

She paused, noticing for the first time how happy he looked to be there. He was basking in the prestige and instant entree their engagment provided. Suddenly the sweet, fruity punch seemed to ferment in her throat. "I think I'll have some champagne after all," she declared.

"I think you need to dance." Taking her hand in his, Brendon led her onto the small dance floor. Surrounded by swaying strangers, beneath the subdued lights, he held her in his arms. The music was soft and low, one sentimental tune after another. As the evening progressed, it became harder to stay angry with him. She blamed it on their romantic surroundings and his dancing expertise.

A while later Emerson cut in. "Talk here is surprisingly in favor of your assuming the presidency of McLean Development," he infomed her, smiling fondly.

A rush of pleasure filled her—until she remembered her commitment to Brendon Sloane. "No conflict of interest?" she asked.

"You and Brendon make an attractive couple. Hopefully, whatever conflict the two firms can't work out in the boardroom you and Brendon can resolve over morning coffee or late-night chats before the fire. And what better way to prove your dedication to remaining in Charleston than by marrying." Not giving her a chance to add a word, he confessed, "I admit I had my doubts. But I can see now that your engagement is for the best. I want you to be happy."

Guilt flooded her. Even the presidency no longer held much appeal. She could only think about the problems she'd caused, the difficulties yet to come.

"Trouble?" Brendon asked, reclaiming her for another dance.

"Only Emerson's complete approval of our engagement."

Brendon studied her wordlessly. "Is that so bad?"

"It just makes it more difficult to let him down. Leveling with my grandfather is going to be very hard." She stared thoughtfully at the guests.

"Then don't," Brendon advised, his eyes darkening with determination. "Because if you do, I'll have to confess, too. And if I lose my financial stake in the Paradise project because of your insensitivity to my needs, I'll have to see that you forfeit, too."

She recalled his threat to go to the local home builders' association, and fury flooded her anew. He seemed not to notice her stiffness as he danced her backward. "You're supposed to look as if you're having a good time," he reminded her with a goading smile. "As if this were the most important night of your life."

"It's the worst," she asserted flatly, stepping deliberately on his toe. "And you want to know who's making it more disgustingly dull?"

Her effort to make him release her failed. He grimaced slightly but didn't relinquish his hold on her or stop waltzing. "You're not the only one who can be clumsy, darling," he warned, his eyes glinting with ill regard. "I'd hate to see you sprawled out on this lovely floor."

She gasped. "You wouldn't!"

"Try me."

The music stopped. Keeping a tight grip on her waist and still smiling, he exchanged pleasantries with other guests near them. When the music started up again, he whirled her sedately around the floor.

"I'd like to stop and have a glass of champagne," she said icily.

His brows lifted at her imperious tone. "The mood you're in, you'd probably get roaring drunk."

That was true. "I'd also like to tour the buffet."

To her surprise, he relented. "I could use some champagne, too." Together but not touching, they strolled toward the buffet table. Savannah felt as if a smile had been glued permanently on her face. Brendon handed her a glass of champagne, and for the first time she noticed that behind the pleasant facade he looked as bored and restless as she was. He tugged at his bow tie. "Tell me, are all these society parties this dull?"

She sipped her champagne, fighting the traitorous warmth she was beginning to feel for him. "Most are worse. When I was seventeen I had to attend one soiree a month. By the time I reached twenty—a delightfully marriagable age— the number was increased to three or four. And the sorority parties at school were even worse."

He regarded her curiously. "Why?"

"Because they were always so frivolous." Beginning to relax, she took another sip of champagne. "I wanted to be doing something important."

"Didn't you ever learn to just have fun?" He moved closer, and her heart thudded uncomfortably at his nearness.

She shook her head. "I had a very sheltered childhood with lots of lessons—dancing, music, riding—but little else in the way of extracurricular activities."

"You've never had fun at one of these gatherings?" Brendon persisted.

She shook her head, growing uneasy at the mischievous glint in his eyes. "What are you thinking?" she whispered.

He removed the glass from her hands. His warm fingers brushed her hands lightly, sending a thrill spiraling through her. "Trust me, darling. We're about to set a precedent," he promised, leading her toward the dance floor.

He wasn't kidding. When the band began another upbeat number, she twined her arms around his neck, struggling to keep up with his swift steps. "Whoa there, partner," she ordered. He was dancing them across the ballroom far too fast, though she was too lightheaded to put up much of a fight. Guests oohed and aahed over their skill. "I'm never going to live this down," she moaned as, without warning, he dipped her nearly to the floor.

"Do you want to?" He held her still. Her hair cascaded over her shoulders. Her back was almost parallel to the floor. She felt like a heroine in an old movie. Emerson had been right; Brendon was a rogue.

"No."

"Know how to tango?"

"Brendon! I don't think the people here are going to appreciate this." She was smiling despite her effort not to.

He shrugged, lifting her to an upright position. The ballroom whirled dizzily. "It's our party."

"So it is."

At the end of the number, he strode over to the orchestra and conferred with the bandleader. A minute later the band broke into a traditional tango. The floor cleared as he took her in his arms. As they glided dramatically from one end of the dance floor to the other, she laughed aloud; she couldn't help it. "I haven't done anything this silly and irresponsible since I was in high school," she admitted breathlessly.

"High time, then, wouldn't you say?" He pressed his cheek close to hers.

"Now all I need is a rose between my teeth."

"Done," Brendon declared.

Their arms extended spectacularly, he danced her toward the vases at the entrance of the ballroom and plucked a red rose for her teeth, a white one to slide beneath the gold clasp in her hair. They resumed the dramatic steps, eyes locking as their bodies adapted to one another's speed and rhythm. She wasn't sure when the music drifted back into a waltz again. She just knew she hadn't felt this way in ages—so free, so abandoned, so young. "I think we're making a spectacle of ourselves," she murmured, not sure she wanted to stop.

Brendon's gaze darkened as he let his eyes drift over her

face. "Engaged couples are given special quarter."

"But we're not engaged!"

His hold on her wrist and waist tightened. "Oh, yes, we are. Much more than you realize."

Emerson appeared unexpectedly. "Savannah, darling, I'm leaving," he informed her.

"Thank you for a lovely party." She leaned forward to give him a kiss.

To her surprise, his eyes misted over. "You don't know what it means to me to have you here with me, Savannah." To Brendon he admonished, "Sloane, behave!"

"Yes, sir!" Brendon snapped a mock two-finger salute, but the grin the two men exchanged aroused Savannah's suspicions. She wondered at the change in their relationship. Was something going on that she didn't know about? Or were they really mending the rift between them?

She watched Emerson depart as she and Brendon moved to the buffet tables, which were loaded with platters of crudités and dips; slices of ham, roast beef, and turkey; assorted cold salads and hot casseroles; rolls; and platters of French pastries and rich cakes for dessert. She munched on a chocolate éclair, relieved to notice that other people were leaving, too.

Brendon helped himself to a plate of sliced roast beef, potato salad, asparagus, and a roll. "It looks as if we convinced the guests what a happy couple we are," he observed.

She froze at his words. Was that why he had danced with her for hours and hours—to convince the guests that they were in love?

She took another gulp of champagne and washed down a mushroom stuffed with sausage. "Perhaps we should nominate you for an Academy Award," she suggested.

Brendon gave her a sharp sidelong glance. "Do you always eat that way? Dessert first, an occasional appetizer later?"

She shrugged. "I stopped having time for regular meals years ago. I learned to eat whatever appealed to me whenever the opportunity presented itself."

His gaze narrowed critically. "Well, your weight has

held, but I'd hate to see an analysis of your blood."

"Very funny."

"It wasn't meant to be."

She sighed and looked away. "Get this straight—you aren't in the least bit responsible for me. I can manage just fine on my own." She helped herself to a bit of clam dip, a sweet-and-sour chicken wing, Alsatian pork with sauerkraut, and orange almond cake.

Brendon glanced critically at her selection. "If that doesn't give you indigestion-induced nightmares, I don't know what will."

She returned his gaze with exasperation. "You worry about your digestion and I'll worry about mine!"

Before Brendon could comment further, the governor appeared to say good-bye. The three of them discussed state property laws, with she and Brendon each knowledgeably holding their own. An endless number of well-wishers followed. Half an hour later they were among the last twenty people present. "Well, that's it." Savannah recalled her decision to tell Emerson everything first thing in the morning. "You're off the hook. Tomorrow you'll be a free man, at least as far as my grandfather and I are concerned." For the sake of their reputations, she knew they'd have to keep up appearances for a short while longer.

"Not necessarily." He strode to the bandstand and said something to the weary orchestra leader. Money exchanged hands discreetly, then the brass struck up a rendition of "If Ever I Would Leave You" just as Brendon returned and took her in his arms. "You may take the lyrics of this song as a direct hint," he announced softly. "I'm not going to let you just walk away from me—not after everything that's happened."

No, she supposed he would want to get his payment via the extra construction work at Paradise first. "A union like ours could hardly be compared to Camelot," she corrected disdainfully, "no matter what you pay the orchestra or how much acting we do in front of other people!"

He folded her more tightly against his chest. "I don't

want you to pretend with me, Savannah. What's it going to take to convince you of that?"

He would have to tell her he loved her, she thought wistfully. He'd have to drop his business demands, end their hoax of an engagement, and begin all over again.

More show tunes followed; all shared the theme of love and all were incredibly romantic. "If you're trying to convince me you have a heart somewhere in that sinewy chest of yours, it's working," she murmured against his solid shoulder. The food and champagne had made her sleepy and all too susceptible to his charms. She struggled to keep the conversation light, adding, "I can hear your heart beating about seventy-five times a minute."

Brendon halted abruptly. His pulse seemed to speed magically beneath her fingertips; his thighs flexed potently against hers. "Count again." Desire, frank and dangerous, flared in his eyes.

"Don't," she said when his lips parted and lowered to her mouth.

"You want me; I want you." His fragrant breath whispered against her brow.

"When I make love with a man again, I want it to be right and meaningful, under mutually caring circumstances," she said softly. "You can't offer me that. This engagement is a game to you, but it's one that will end, make no mistake about it."

He frowned but didn't pursue the argument. Instead he helped himself calmly to a third glass of icy champagne. The band departed shortly thereafter. Brendon tipped the manager of the club, retrieved her wrap, and escorted her outside. She shivered in the cool January air. She should have brought a coat.

Brendon held the car door for her then sprinted around the front and hopped in, turning on the motor and the heater. Icy air assaulted Savannah's already shivering form.

"Cold?" he asked, shooting her an amused sidelong glance as he continued to adjust the knobs.

"Like an icicle." She was trembling from head to toe.

"Well, we can't have that." He slid across the seat and took her ruthlessly into his arms. His head bent to hers and stifled the protest automatically forming on her lips. "I'll warm you up in no time," he promised.

His kiss sent fire licking through her limbs. "There should be a penalty for tactics like this," she murmured, pushing at his wide shoulders.

Air gushed out the vents, further heating the car. "There is. Five hours of dancing with you," Brendon murmured, teasingly licking her lips. "With not a bedroom or sofa or quiet broom closet in sight." Considering the degree of his arousal, she guessed that even their present setting would have done. But she had no intention of making love in the front seat of a car. "Brendon!" She pushed firmly against his chest.

"Later," he murmured, his lips brushing her mouth. The tickling sensation robbed her of breath and the will to resist him. "After this." A torrent of hot, feverish kisses rained down on her mouth. As her lips parted beneath the insistent pressure, he shifted closer. "I've wanted to take that dress off all night," he murmured against her shoulders, his lips following the jersey neckline to trace her skin. "I want to see what you're wearing beneath it." His hands closed around the firm curve of her hip and slid beneath her to pull her determinedly onto his lap.

The car was quite warm, but it was cool compared to the heat of his kiss, of his hands moving reverently over her. She knew she should resist, but the tenderness underlying his kiss destroyed her determination to remain aloof. She gave herself up utterly to his embrace, laced her hands behind his neck, and slid her fingers through his hair. Brendon reacted instantaneously. His hand slid over her wildly pounding heart, cupped a breast, and caressed a peaking nipple.

Abruptly, as if with great effort, he pulled back. His hands fell from her shoulders, and he fastened his fingers resolutely around the steering wheel. "I promised Emerson this morning that we'd be more discreet," he said, obviously cursing the words. His expression became more closed. "I can't take you home, and my place is equally public."

His blunt words destroyed whatever romantic notions she had. He wanted to take her to bed, she reminded herself firmly, ignoring the knife twist of hurt. He wanted to use her to get back at Emerson and McLean Development, to wreak havoc on her for ever attempting to use him.

"A motel is out of the question," she said icily, her coldness meant to cover the hurt and aching embarrassment she felt for having succumbed to his advances. "A sexual liaison is out of the question."

His jaw dropped in amazement, then turned rigid with fury. "And what the hell was that just now?" he demanded. "What did you intend when you selected that particular dress? Don't tell me you don't know how sexy you look! Or how it was bound to affect me!"

She felt a pang of regret. She *had* unintentionally led him on several times previously, only to panic when their embrace became more intimate. But she wouldn't let him use her guilt to push her into a disastrous affair. "All my formal gowns are sexy!" She shot back angrily. "As for this one, I selected it at random. The dress, like the party, was just window dressing for the scam, a means to an end, a way to become president." She surprised herself with the calculated dispassion her anger allowed her to feign. "I used you, Brendon, just like you're trying to use me now!"

He gazed furiously at her. His hand rested motionlessly on the seat behind her, but she had the uncomfortable feeling he was fighting the urge to prove her a liar. "Well, I'll say this for you, sweetheart," he retorted. "You give the word *calculated* new depth and meaning." He moved behind the wheel and shifted the Mercedes into reverse.

She leaned her head wearily against the window as he drove. Part of her yearned to correct the impression she'd just given. Another part of her wanted to keep the hard core of deceit wrapped around her as protection from him and the growing prospect of falling in love with him. Because if nothing else, the evening had proved beyond a shadow of a doubt that she was dangerously close to it.

Her dark lashes lowered as he continued to navigate the

winding country roads along the shore. She sighed, stifling a deep yawn. The next thing she knew the car was coming to a stop. But they weren't in front of the McLean's Charleston mansion or her adjacent carriage house. She shook herself awake. "Where are we?"

"Kiawah Motor Inn." Brendon parked in a space across from the lighted lobby. A neon light flickered No Vacancies above them. Relief flooded her when she realized they couldn't possibly stay there. Anger followed.

"Why are we stopping here?" she demanded icily. It took every bit of her inner fortitude to remain calm.

"I don't know about you"—Brendon smiled tightly as he yanked the keys from the ignition and pocketed them resolutely—"but I'd like a little sleep."

"But the country club's only half an hour from home!" she asserted grimly, her temper rising.

"If you're going north." Brendon opened his door and got out. "We've been going south. And Kiawah Island is another thirty minutes in the opposite direction, which puts us an hour's drive from Charleston."

She would kill him. "We can't go in there like this." She gestured at their elegant evening attire. "It's two in the morning! We don't have any luggage." She pointed to the blinking sign above. "And they don't have any rooms."

"I reserved mine earlier." His brows raised in mock concern. "Are you coming?"

Of all the arrogant nerve! "No!" She huddled even closer into her glittery black evening wrap and felt blindly for the sandals she'd kicked off earlier.

"Suit yourself, but it's going to be one heck of a long, cold night—and I've got the car keys." The door slammed shut on the expletive hissing through her teeth.

She watched him saunter across the parking lot toward the welcoming lights of the lobby. Damn him, she thought, hobbling out of the car after him. Inelegantly she bent to slip on her other shoe. He turned and grinned, hands shoved in his pockets, and waited for her to catch up.

"I'm going to get you for this one, Brendon," she muttered under her breath.

"You might *attempt* to even the score." Whistling, he

entered the brightly lit room, teasing Savannah to stagger after him. If he'd meant to make her pay for her earlier remarks and subsequent rejection, he was succeeding.

She fought the urge to ask the clerk when the next bus was leaving for Charleston. If worse came to worse, she could sit in the lobby all night. She certainly wasn't going to call Emerson and ask for a ride home. If only she knew how, she would hot wire Brendon's car.

"Good evening, folks." The desk clerk grinned from ear to ear as he took in the formal attire. Savannah sank down on a chair, still struggling with her delicate sandal strap. She knew her hair was still mussed, her lipstick gone and her lips red from kissing. Her cheeks felt flushed, and she felt guilty as sin and all of seventeen years old. Her glittery black shawl could not cover the low cut of her dress, and Brendon made no attempt to hide his amused come-hither stare.

He lounged indolently against the front desk. "I made reservations earlier."

The clerk struggled to keep his face expressionless. "Name?"

"George Washington Carver, Mr. and Mrs." Brendon's broad shoulders lifted in an apologetic shrug. She could see the goading excuse mirrored in his eyes. He had promised Emerson he would be more discreet.

Her teeth clenched in embarrassment. The clerk was laughing so hard he could hardly stand up. "Yes sir, Mr. Carver, we'll have that reservation in just a moment, if you'll just fill out this card."

"We'll pay cash in advance." Brendon scribbled obligingly and produced the appropriate bills. Savannah hid her face in her hands. The ruthless, honorless cad!

The formalities complete, Brendon tapped her shoulder and grinned merrily down at her. "Ready?"

With difficulty she saved her spicy retort for another time. "Do I have a choice?"

"Not if you intend to be as discreet as I intend to be."

"Sir, may I help you with your luggage?" the clerk inquired.

Brendon assumed a guileless expression. "We don't have

any." He opened the door, palm up, to lead her into the cool night air.

"I ought to kill you, Brendon Sloane," she swore once they were outside. "Take a knife to the center of your villainous Yankee heart and—"

"Tsk, tsk." He clucked reprovingly as he directed her around the pool toward the two-story rectangular structure of dark motel rooms. "If there's one thing you've got to remember in the business world, sweetheart, it's to keep a cool head at all times and never say anything you don't fully intend to follow through on."

"And I suppose you're the model businessman."

"When it comes to going after what I want, you'd better believe it." He stopped in front of Room 103. "I believe this is yours."

He rattled the keys in his palm. A second one read Room 204. She blushed even more fiercely. "You planned this," she stammered at last. "Even before I turned you down."

He nodded.

"And asked for two separate rooms?"

"On different floors."

"Why?"

"The Paradise project is only a few miles away. We're touring it tomorrow so I can assess what needs to be done and give you a good estimate on how long it will take and how much of a crew will be needed."

She glared furiously at him. But she saw at once the practicality of the situation. As long as she was here, she might as well take advantage of his proximity and expertise. "I'll accept an estimate from you, but I won't guarantee the work will be assigned to your firm."

"Fair enough."

"But I don't have any clothes."

"I'll drop off something appropriate in the morning."

Her rage at being coerced into spending the night surfaced again at his obvious premeditation. "I'm not going to forgive you for this, Brendon," she muttered in a low voice.

He laughed softly, then leaned forward to take her by

the shoulders and plant the softest, most unthreatening kiss on her brow. "Yes, you will, Savannah. And sooner than you think."

CHAPTER
Eleven

THE INSISTENT RINGING of the phone woke Savannah early the next morning. She grappled for the receiver and pulled it to her ear. "Morning sweetheart," a soft voice drawled.

"Brendon." She moaned, burrowing deeper under the covers. Across the room her black evening gown hung on a hanger. She'd rinsed out her stockings and panties in the bathroom sink and hung them on the shower stall to dry. Crisp sheets moved sensuously across her flesh as she pulled the phone into her bed. "What time is it?" Beyond the drapes she could see only darkness.

"Five A.M. You sound sleepy."

"I am." Her tone was heavy with sarcasm. In contrast, he sounded remarkably cheerful, his voice intensely low and male. A shiver of desire engulfed her as she recalled the way he had kissed her the previous evening.

"Comfortable night?" he inquired.

"Yes," she answered tersely.

"Bed all right?"

She stretched languidly. "It's very cozy," she replied coolly.

"What are you wearing?"

She paused, then shrugged and admitted honestly, "My diamond ring." He laughed, the sexy sound sending a ripple of pleasure down her spine.

"What are *you* wearing?" she asked boldly, lured by the safety of their respective locations.

"Less."

She was appalled to find heat flooding her cheeks. Damn the man! He'd broken through her reserve again.

"Going back to sleep on me?" he prodded tenderly.

She moaned. It was only a phone conversation, yet he had her on fire with desire. "I wish."

"Good. I'll be right over. Your clothes are outside your door."

"Brendon—"

"If you want a shower, get one now." The phone went dead. Savannah stared angrily at it. The thought of the scene Brendon would make if she didn't follow his instructions prompted her to get up. Mentally she envisioned guests piling out of neighboring rooms, angry at being disturbed by the commotion he'd make pounding on her door. She didn't want that.

The bag outside her door contained a hooded stadium sweater in soft winter wheat, a matching silk shirt, designer jeans, heavy cotton socks, lacy white panties embroidered with tiny red hearts, and a lacy front-clasp bra of transparent white. A pair of heavy construction-style boots completed the outfit. In addition, he'd included a toothbrush and toothpaste, antiperspirant, and a small vial of her brand of perfume. Aware that he'd arrive at any moment, she showered and dressed quickly. She was lacing the second boot when a knock sounded at her door.

She let him in. His eyes brightened as he surveyed her. "Right perfume?" he inquired.

"Who helped you?" She folded her evening clothes into the department store bag.

"Emerson's housekeeper. I told her I needed your sizes for a trousseau."

"How clever."

"I thought so." Before she could step back, his arms closed around her and his mouth stole the breath from her. Her instinctive protest was lost in the persistent demand of his probing lips. Despite her resentment, she stepped closer and let him fit his body more closely to hers. She reveled in the girded strength of his thighs pressing against hers.

Thoughts of what he had done to her the evening before fled. She only knew how he made her feel now—exquisite, cherished, a woman newly discovered. And, God help her, she wanted it to continue. Her breasts pressed against his chest. She tasted the minty traces of toothpaste in his searching, searing mouth. His arm circled her tightly and moved up her back to splay possessively across her shoulderblades. The other hand wove through her hair, then dropped to her shoulders, collarbone, and breasts. The warmth of the sweater over the silk blouse was nothing compared to the scorching heat of his hand as he caressed her through her clothes. She felt her nipples bud into tight knots of desire, and she surged against him, a purr of frustration sounding in her throat. He whispered her name as she breathed raggedly against his mouth.

Brendon held her closer, his lips trailing from her mouth to her ear. He buried his face in her hair. As their breathing slowed, he gripped her fiercely to him, then let her go. "We've got a long day ahead of us. I want to reach the site before dawn."

Back to business as usual, she thought. She should have been relieved he hadn't seduced her, but she felt only disappointment. How could he exert such control? Did he care that much for her . . . or that little?

The Paradise construction site was covered with dust and crowded with trucks. More than one helmeted head rose as Savannah alighted from Brendon Sloane's car. Her fiancé strode effortlessly beside her, pausing to say a brief but congenial hello to the foreman and a few of the men. She ignored their speculative glances.

"I don't mind showing you around our new development," she said. "Emerson brought several people from the local home builders' association out for a cursory tour just last week. But don't expect any favoritism when it comes to the bids for the extra work. Our relationship will have no bearing on which firm gets the additional subcontracting."

Brendon's brows rose as he helped her over a section of wood planking. The foundations for all three hundred condominiums had been laid. Wooden frames had been erected and the bulk of the insulation tacked on. Where the ground had been cleared, thick mud pooled in a dark brown sea. Toward the coast highway stood a thick strand of magnolia and cottonwood trees. Toward the shore was marshland and drifting sand dunes. A green belt of common lawn would be laid as soon as the major construction was completed. "Do you have any of the units finished?" Brendon asked. "I'd like to see what the condos will look like inside." When she hesitated, he added, "The floor plans are already on file with the zoning commission."

"All right, but this is it. I really insist you take me back to town as soon as we're through here."

"Agreed."

She led the way to the model on the far side of the complex. He stalked obediently beside her, his long strides threatening to overpower hers with every step. Inside, he surveyed the ivory carpet, the semiglossed walls, the wood-burning fireplace, vaulted ceiling, private redwood deck, and breathtaking view of the ocean. Finally he let out a dissatisfied sigh. "Your interiors are too standard," he pronounced grimly. "They'll never sell."

She gasped in amazement. Her glance traveled from the well-equipped kitchen to the loft-style second floor, oversize master bedroom, bath, and whirlpool. Brendon continued to inspect the workmanship as he talked. "You need ceiling fans, skylights, and indoor grills."

"All those amenities can be added at the time of purchase," Savannah said. "We're trying to keep the base price down as much as possible."

Brendon cast her a speculative look. "Sloane Construction offers those features in all its custom-built homes. You should, too, if you want to be at all competitive with what we're building in town."

"McLean doesn't have the funds to do that and build the golf course, restaurant, and mini shopping mall as well."

"Forget the funds for a moment. Let's concentrate on what's ultimately possible. Most of your units are still in the slab stage. With some quick adjustments on the blueprints and specifications by my architectural department, you could add greenhouse windows, hot tubs, dining room credenzas, built-in kitchen desks, and bookshelves. Even an electric garage door opener in each unit. The cost to McLean would be negligible compared to what it would cost the individual homeowners to purchase the materials and contract for the additional labor. It would also greatly enhance the salability of each unit. Market research has shown that only two major age groups are buying oceanfront property, Savannah—retirees and the career-minded twenty-four-to-thirty-five age group. And if they can afford this, they can afford the luxuries. They also want them installed without undue difficulty."

She knew that what he was saying was true, but McLean couldn't afford all that. "Given the choice between luxurious interiors and group facilities, I think we'd be better off going with the clubhouse and providing the exterior ambience first."

"Why not provide both?"

She sighed. "Because we don't have the funds."

"I'll finance the interiors as well as provide the labor crews," Brendon offered. "We'll let our lawyers work out a split in the profits."

She shook her head. "Emerson would never agree to it." Besides, she wanted sole credit for the Paradise project. She'd worked too hard to accept anything less.

"You're making a mistake," Brendon said quietly.

"That's my option, isn't it?"

Brendon was silent during the drive back to town. He parked in front of her carriage house as promised and strolled with her to the door. He lounged patiently against the door frame as she rummaged through her purse for her keys. "Have dinner with me tonight at my place," he suggested softly.

She paused, her heart pounding. He moved closer until his warm breath was brushing her hair. With effort she kept her voice light. "Don't you think we've played out this practical joke?"

"Yes, I do." The seriousness of his gaze made her heart pound even faster. "But since our engagement party was just last night, I don't think it's the correct time to confess. And I do want to spend time with you. I want us to have a real date, Savannah, all this engagement nonsense aside." His lips brushed her temple softly. She, too, wanted to spend time with him.

"All right," she agreed finally. "But I'll drive." That way she could see herself home at her own leisure.

He grinned. "Be there at seven."

Weak-kneed, she watched him walk to his car. The cadence of his confident step echoed in her mind long after he had left.

Minutes later Savannah had changed into a white wool business suit with a cardigan jacket and a rose silk shirt with a high-banded collar and buttons down the front. She drove to work and stopped at the reception desk to pick up her mail. As she strode happily toward her office, she was halted by an unexpected but familiar male voice. Without warning Emerson opened his office door. "Savannah, we were just talking about you."

Her inquisitive gaze met Brendon's gleaming eyes. A rueful smile tugged at his mouth. She noted that he hadn't taken time to change. He still wore the same jeans, flannel shirt, and leather jacket he'd had on that morning. "You didn't tell me you planned to see Emerson," she said. Brendon only smiled.

Emerson led her into his office and shut the door before Brendon could reply. "Sloane told me what you've been working on this morning. I must say I'm impressed. Upgrading the project would be good for both firms. I have no objection to Brendon's firm underwriting the cost and labor of the extra interior features—for a *small* percentage of the profit, directly proportional to the final asking price. Naturally we'll let our financial geniuses haggle out the details, but I would guess roughly five to ten percent of the profits would be fair."

Savannah was outraged that Brendon had gone behind her back. "The project is still mine," she insisted. "I alone have the power to hire and fire as I see fit."

Emerson nodded. "But Brendon told me you were concerned about my feelings. I want you to know that I have no objection."

"How nice," she murmured, shooting Brendon a malevolent look.

He stepped forward, his eyes never leaving her face. "Of course the major credit for the complex will still go to McLean Development. The public doesn't need to know Sloane Construction had anything to do with it, if that's what you decide. I'm well aware that it's your project, Savannah."

He didn't act that way, she thought furiously. "And it will be a way of putting some of your people back to work," Emerson added, sending Brendon a respectful glance.

Savannah turned to Brendon in surprise. "You've laid off people?"

He frowned. "Not yet but we've been cutting it close. This work comes in the nick of time for a lot of my men. I've been wondering what I was going to do."

Knowing that the reason behind Brendon's covert moves was concern for his employees made some of her anger dissipate.

"Well, Savannah, if you don't mind, I think I'll go on to my luncheon meeting," Emerson said. "I promised to meet with Harve about the new lower rate financing we're trying to obtain."

Brendon's head lifted in silent acknowledgment. "Let me know how it goes, Emerson. A new package from the bank could give us all a boost."

"Will do," Emerson promised, shutting the door softly behind him.

Savannah turned angrily back to Brendon. "Well, you've certainly got him eating out of the palm of your hand," she said, throwing her mail onto Emerson's desk.

Brendon slouched casually against the wall, his arms crossed negligently over his chest. "Just two hours ago you implied that the only thing standing in the way of Sloane Construction taking over the subcontracting was Emerson's dislike of me. So I took care of it. I thought you'd prefer not to be here in case it went the other way."

"You could have told me about it first," she asserted angrily.

"Would you have agreed to let me approach him?"

"No! And what goes on between Emerson and me is our business!"

"Wrong, Savannah." Brendon straightened, towering over her, his jaw clenched. "You made it my business when you asked me to intervene, to take part in this scam of yours. Now I'm in it. I saw a way my firm could benefit; I took it. We'll all come out the better."

Her anger remained. "I'll investigate other firms, Brendon, and get additional bids. Regardless of what Emerson said to you just now, the final decision is still mine."

He gave her a hard, assessing look. "Sloane Construction is the only firm that can handle it, Savannah. And you won't get a better price for the quality of the work. However, if you need to find that out for yourself, so be it. Just remember whose idea the additional amenities were, and be aware that I have other ideas, too. Ideas I didn't and won't share until we sign the papers assigning the subcontracting to my firm." He headed toward the door, looking just as angry as she felt.

"I suppose this cancels that dinner invitation you issued

earlier," she added tautly, for some reason feeling disappointed. She had wanted to see him, despite their disagreements.

He smiled. "On the contrary. Unless, of course, you're afraid to come."

She bristled at the challenge in his voice. "Don't be ridiculous."

"I'll see you this evening, then. And Savannah," he cautioned, "don't be late." She stared after him in vexation. Would she ever get him out of her heart and mind?

CHAPTER
Twelve

SAVANNAH SPENT THE rest of the day on the phone investigating other construction firms in the area. Time and again Brendon's words came back to haunt her. She knew the ideas for improving the interiors of the condominiums had been his. She knew from studying his firm's history in Charleston that he was a financial and contracting genius. The only advantages he lacked were occasional capital and aristocratic connections. She had both. She didn't have the crews to do what needed to be done at Paradise and still make an April first opening date. Working with his firm would benefit them both. Why, then, was she so reluctant? Because she didn't want to share the glory if Paradise was a success? Or because she didn't want Brendon to want her only because of the additional work her firm could provide?

Either way, she had to see him, if only to understand her own raging desire for him. Promptly at seven she arrived at his town house.

"I wasn't sure you'd come," he said, ushering her inside.

His gaze made a leisurely tour of her body.

Tilting her head regally, she refused to admit how much she'd wanted to be with him. "We had a date," she said. "I don't know why you'd think I wouldn't honor that."

Inside, everything glowed with readiness. A fire burned neatly in the hearth. Candles, silver, and china were arranged on the table. A bottle of champagne was chilling on ice. A tray of tempting raw vegetables and sour-cream dip was on the coffee table.

Brendon wore a soft black herringbone jacket and black flannel slacks. His white cotton shirt was crisply starched, his tie made of expensive black silk. The fact that he'd apparently showered and shaved just for her set her emotions awhirl. How long had it been since anyone had cared enough about her to go to even half that trouble?

The dinner was delicious. As the meal ended, Brendon poured them each more champagne. His eyes held hers for a passionate moment. She sought to steer the conversation onto safe ground. "How did you get involved in the construction business?" she asked. "Was it a lifelong ambition? Part of the family trade?"

He shook his head. "My father died when I was a kid, and my mother worked nights in a factory, so we didn't have much money."

"I'm sorry."

"Don't be. If anything, it made me stronger. I worked my way through college on a construction gang, primarily because it paid well. The last two years I was able to go to school full-time using money I had saved, but that meant cutting expenses to the bone. That's when I learned how to cook." He grinned. "I lived off campus. When I got tired of oatmeal and peanut butter, I followed a budget column in the newspaper on how to live on ten dollars a week. I kept at it until I was an expert on meatless pasta dishes and meals for one. I learned how to cut recipes to exactly the proportion I needed, make dinners and freeze them so I wouldn't have to cook during exams."

"Bachelor survival?" she asked teasingly, admiring his gumption.

He grimaced ruefully. "It was either that or do without heat, and I had my priorities."

"What about girls? Did you date?"

He sighed. "Not many girls my age were interested in being with a guy who studied all hours of the night and day, so no, I didn't. Later, when I could afford to date, I mentally reviewed each candidate, imagining them in the bare apartments of my college days. None of them passed the test. And if they weren't capable of roughing it, then they weren't ready to live with me."

She thought of how she must have appeared to him. He'd worked for everything in life. In comparison she'd had it all handed to her on a silver platter. "When did you begin your business?"

Brendon poured them more champagne. "After college I went to work for a large engineering firm. I realized that I liked being outdoors more than in a stuffy office building, and I also wanted to be my own boss. So I quit my job and began subcontracting. By working eighteen- and twenty-hour days and taking a lot of small jobs no one else would touch, I was able to build a successful firm. Later I renovated old apartment buildings and sold them as condominiums. When the recession hit, I moved here."

The record on the stereo flicked off. Brendon rose reluctantly. "If you'll tend to the stereo," he said, "I'll clear the table."

Savannah selected a mix of soft ballads and rock. He joined her several minutes later. His hands slid around her waist and he pulled her to him. While they danced together in the semi-darkness, his glance flickered over her silk camisole, matching scarlet wool trousers, and dolman-sleeve silver-threaded scarlet jacket. "You're so beautiful," he whispered. "Everything I could ever want."

His kiss was no surprise. His tongue ravished her sweetly. Desire was a limitless wellspring within her, surpassed only by her need to be loved. His light touch on her arms seemed not nearly intimate enough. Her hands laced around his neck and trailed impatiently across his shoulders, down his shirt front to his waist. A purr of contentment sounded in his throat. As he held her tightly against him, the thudding of his heart seemed to mirror hers. "Savannah, Savannah," he whispered, "you're the one woman I've met who could have survived my destitute college days, who would have come out the stronger for it. I need you with me tonight. Stay with me, please."

Her palms splayed across his chest. "Brendon..." She tilted her head back to scrutinize his face. The reasons why she shouldn't stay fled. "I need you, too," she whispered.

His mouth curved lovingly over hers and his tongue swept her mouth repeatedly, as if drinking in the sweetness. Hot waves of longing surged through her, weakening her knees. She leaned into his embrace, wanting to assuage the ache deep within her. She wanted to know him intimately, to glory in his love.

Brendon seemed equally driven. His hands slid to her waist. Still kissing her, swaying to the last romantic strains of low music, he slid his fingers into the waistband of her slacks. Inch by inch he pulled the silky camisole free. Cool air assaulted her skin moments before his searching hands made a gentle but thorough foray up her spine. She trembled at the passion racking her. Her hands curled more tightly around his neck. Instinctively she aligned herself to the muscular contours of his lean length, pressing her soft breasts into his solid chest.

A low groan escaped Brendon's throat as he broke off the kiss and buried his face in her hair. "Sweet... sweet heaven," he whispered. "Paradise." And then his mouth was on hers again, claiming, plundering, evoking rush after rush of tempestuous sensations. Her nipples had tightened into buds of longing. His hands found the pebble-hard tips and massaged them slowly, lingeringly, through the thin layer of silk. "You're so warm, Savannah." She was burning, flaming for him.

Wordlessly he drew the quilted jacket from her shoulders. His fingers traced the lace edge of her camisole, brushed her swelling breasts. His eyes were dark, his hands warm on her bare shoulders. Slowly he edged the thin straps from her shoulders and down her arms. Deliberately indolent movements exposed her skin to his rapacious gaze. He lowered the fabric just short of the dusky rose centers of her breasts and trailed a contemplative finger past her collarbone to her lips. Then his mouth closed over hers.

"Sweet, sweet Savannah," he whispered, merging his lips and tongue with hers. He kissed her gently and tenderly before finally pulling back. She was trembling with impatience, her arms twined tightly around his shoulders.

"I want to make love to you," Brendon said softly. "Tell me it's what you want, too. I won't go on unless you're sure."

She knew then that she was in love with him. He lifted her face to his. His gentle touch, his compelling gaze, drove the breath from her lungs. "I want you more than life itself," she whispered. She would never forget, never regret...

He held her away from him for long seconds, as if committing her features to memory. And then he was kissing her again, deeply, passionately, taking her into a whirlpool of desire so intense it was impossible to think, to breathe. Abruptly his arm was beneath her knees and she was swung into the air and held against his chest. He took the stairs two at a time, his gaze never leaving her face.

He strode to the bedroom and set her down wordlessly at the side of the bed. His cologne scenting the room added a dizzying dimension to her spiraling senses. Savannah watched him shrug out of his jacket, then helped him with his tie and the first several buttons of his shirt. She halted shyly at the waist. His hand covered hers encouragingly as he helped her tug the material from the waistband of his slacks. "You're beautiful," he whispered. The back of his hand brushed her jaw.

"So are you."

"And so soft." He lifted a wrist for her help. Her fingers trembled as she undid one cuff link, then the other. Brendon pulled her close for a long kiss. "We've got all the time in the world," he murmured, holding her close.

"I know."

"And so much to learn about loving each other." He shrugged out of his shirt and tossed it to the floor, kicked off his shoes, then his socks. His trousers slid down to lie with the rest of his clothes.

The straps of her camisole lay halfway across her arms. Gently he lowered the silk until it fell free of her breasts. His palms encompassed the soft creamy globes, kneading and caressing. Savannah drifted with the sensations he was evoking. Her mouth opened to his hungry kiss. Her hands wove through the silky mat of light brown hair on his chest. She found the flat nipples, the contours of solid male flesh. And then they were clinging together, her nipples brushing his chest in a wealth of glorious sensation. Brendon groaned and clutched her more tightly to him. "You're wanton, Savannah," he teased.

In answer she moved against him, intensifying the pleasure for them both. His desire was a steel rod pressing between her trousered legs. Brendon reached for the front fastening of her slacks and undid her belt as his mouth made a leisurely tour of her breasts. He kissed his way down to her navel and kneeled to help her step out of the slacks. Both hands made a tantalizingly slow journey up the curve of each leg, past her knees, to her thighs. When he reached her lacy panties, she gasped audibly. He pressed tiny kisses along the inside of her thighs, his fingers sliding beneath the elastic. She gripped his shoulders tightly, relaxing only slightly when he removed the scrap of cloth from her hips.

Brendon's hands wrapped around her tightly. His lips made the wetness between her thighs more intense. Her body arched in readiness and she bit her lip to stifle a cry of passion. His hands roamed over her thighs, her abdomen, her breasts. "Brendon, please..." she whispered. Kneeling with him, she learned his hard male contours for the very first time and shamelessly divested him of the brief white scrap of cloth.

"I don't want to hurt you," he whispered against her hair, holding her possessively.

"I want you," she whispered.

"You're sure?" Earnestly he searched her face as his hands blazed a new fiery trail of exquisite sensations.

"Absolutely." Savannah groaned and impatiently tumbled him back onto his bed. They landed in a laughing, tangled heap of arms and legs. But their amusement faded fast as the length of his hard male body was stretched out over hers.

"Savannah?"

"Now." His hair-roughened thigh parted hers, his gentle, searching finger eased the way to make the joining complete. She pressed tightly against him, savoring every moment. His mouth encompassed hers sweetly, swiftly, and they moved together provocatively, fiercely, gently. She arched into him, holding him closer, whispering his name. And then all thought was lost as the need built inside her. She moved to his steady rhythm. She rocked against him, receded, arched, in need of the fulfillment just out of her reach. Her cry of passion was stifled by the demanding ardor of his mouth. Her breasts and thighs were soothed by the knowing ministrations of his hands. And then there was nothing but him and her, and the pleasure, and the driving passion engulfing, then satiating them both.

Long afterward they lay together, her head on his chest. Savannah listened to his heart thumping steadily and reveled in the warm strength of his arms around her. "What are you thinking?" Brendon's voice was low and affectionate as he stroked her back.

That I love you, she thought. More completely and tenderly than I have ever loved any man. But she couldn't say it out loud. "We're good together, you and I," she said cautiously, softly.

Brendon raised himself on an elbow. He glanced down at her, a frown twisting his beautiful mouth. She arched against him contentedly, letting a slow, sultry gaze and ardent smile convey the affection she couldn't yet put into words. He relaxed.

His arm tightened around her as he pulled her closer into his embrace. His fingers tangled loosely in her dark hair. "It feels good having you here," he admitted. "As if it was meant to be." She nodded. "I want you to spend the night with me," he urged very low. "I know what we said about being discreet, but . . ." His voice caught huskily in his throat. Her eyes shut as she savored every hard male inch of his naked body. "I want to stay, too." She snuggled closer, not knowing when she had ever felt so complete, so at peace.

Abruptly Brendon rolled over so that she was beneath him. His forearms lay flat against the pillow on either side of her head. His lips nipped tiny kisses at the corners and then the center of her mouth. "I care about you, Savannah," he confessed. "I don't want anything to come between us—not work, not the engagement, not our backgrounds, as different as they are."

"I want to be with you, too," she admitted. But thoughts of the future were lost with the knowing ministrations of his hands. "Brendon," she murmured, shifting to allow him better access to a full, pointing breast.

"My thoughts exactly," he whispered against her pliant mouth. "The night is young, Savannah, and there's so much yet to be tried . . ."

Her hands curved against his shoulders as he slowly slid his body back down the length of hers, his tongue making tantalizing forays over every silken inch of her. She arched against him, trembling wildly, a low moan torn from the back of her throat. Brendon laughed softly and triumphantly as he slid back her prone length.

She rolled onto him, her total abandonment in the heat of passion surprising her almost as much as it seemed to stun and please him. "You make me feel reckless," she whispered, her hands cupping his hard male heat. "Powerful, fulfilled, and every inch a woman." Her lips paid homage to the skin her hands had caressed. Brendon groaned, shifting her so that their lengths were more comfortably aligned. And then he was moving over her again, pulsing, hot, hard, and demanding.

"I want you," he whispered. "More than I've ever wanted a woman." Her flesh was a silken sheath for his passion. Kisses and caresses blended into one; the ecstasy of their joining overrode all else.

They still clung together a long time later. Savannah was shaken into a silence that was complete and encompassing. For the first time in her life she felt utterly content.

CHAPTER
Thirteen

THE PLEASANT AROMA of coffee stirred Savannah into wakefulness. She stretched in the mussed warmth of cocoa-brown sheets and glanced over where Brendon had slept. A feeling of cozy well-being came over her as she recalled the passion of the previous night.

Yawning, she rose from the bed and pulled on his hooded blue robe. She found him in the upstairs study, seated in front of a computer terminal reading the fluorescent green data printed on the video screen. He'd pulled on a pair of worn jeans. A faded blue chambray work shirt clung to his shoulders, unbuttoned partway down his chest. Savannah longed to run her fingers through the springy mat of hair on his chest. "Come over here and give me a hug, woman," he said with a teasing grin.

Flushing, she draped an arm around his shoulders and bestowed a quick kiss on the top of his head. He pulled her onto his lap. The scent of their lovemaking still clung to him. The golden bristles of his morning beard tickled her skin. "Mmm, you feel good," he whispered.

"So do you," she admitted.

He held her fiercely, his face nestled in the soft contours of his robe between Savannah's breasts. Her nipples tautened in response. She was conscious of the exposed swell of flesh open to his ardent gaze, the warmth of his breath on her feverish skin.

"I was going to let you sleep," he said. His hand slid into the neckline of the robe and traced a fiery line down to her waist. Her insides melted in response. But the next instant he was squeezing her affectionately again and turning back toward the terminal screen. She sighed with disappointment, stood, and stretched. She'd distract him from his work later, she decided. Perhaps when he was ready for his morning shower.

"What are you doing?" She pulled up a nearby chair. He certainly seemed engrossed.

"Checking out the location of my crews. If we're going to get started on Paradise, I've got some rearranging to do."

A tight knot of tension formed in her stomach. "Brendon, the deal between our two companies isn't set yet." She took a deep breath. "Considering our involvement, I don't think we can work together."

He flicked off the computer and faced her. "Who is it you don't trust, Savannah? Me or yourself?"

"Brendon . . ." She flushed, appalled that he had read her thoughts so well.

"I didn't make love with you last night to seal any deal with McLean, if that's what you're thinking. I won't lie to you, though. The loss of the Paradise project hurt my firm badly. I need that extra work. My company won't survive without it."

"If I give you the work, I'll be accused of favoritism."

"Then let Emerson award it," he said harshly. "Relinquish your control of the project and let him give the contracting to whatever firm he deems capable."

She stood, resenting him for putting her in such a difficult

position. "I've had a hard time establishing myself in the
construction business," she said carefully. "My mother was
appalled by my choice of profession. My grandfather in-
dulged me but didn't take me seriously. He still doesn't.
He wants me married, for heaven's sake! If I were a man,
he wouldn't be making such outrageous demands, but because I'm a woman, he perceives me as weak and needing
male guidance and care. If I give up control of the project
because of you, I'll be proving him right. I can't let anything
interfere with this. If I do, my career will be ruined."

His jaw tautened. He glanced at the clock. Savannah
noted that it was already seven. They were due at their
respective offices in another hour or so. "We'll talk about
it during breakfast," Brendon decided.

Knowing it was pointless to argue about the work or their
relationship, she nodded. Then, in an uncharacteristically
evasive action, she waited until he was in the shower, dressed
quickly, went downstairs, and slipped out the door.

Savannah spent the morning continuing her search for
another firm to do the subcontracting on Paradise. Locally
there was no one outfit capable of handling all the work.
To call in a firm from the northern part of the state meant
paying compensatory lodgings, food, and travel expenses.
And McLean didn't have the extra money, even if she came
up with a justifiable reason to spend it, which she couldn't.
"You're getting as irrational as Emerson used to be on the
subject of Sloane Construction," John Crawford commented
when he dropped by her office.

"Sloane tends to assume control," she said. "I can't see
him willingly taking orders from me." He could also make
mincemeat out of her with just one sultry look. How could
she function in such an overcharged atmosphere? And these
were no penny-ante stakes. This was a multimillion-dollar
deal, on which the whole future of McLean Development
depended.

"It's a McLean project. Sloane understands that," John
countered reasonably. "Regardless of who does the subcontracting, the project will carry our firm's name."

It would also have the stamp of Brendon's creativity, if he had his way. And she had counted on the Paradise project to prove her worth. If she shared the credit, she'd never know if she could make it on her own.

The carriage house looked bleakly empty as Savannah parked her Cadillac in front. It had proved a long, fruitless day, and tension made her shoulders ache as she fit her key into the lock. Unfortunately she still had a long night ahead of her. Both her arms and her briefcase were full of possible advertising plans for Paradise. They required a decision soon, too.

She kicked open the door, entered, and closed it with a backward prod of her toe. "How do I ever get myself into these messes?" she asked out loud.

"Good question." Startled by the male voice she jumped, dropping several folders. "Maybe if you acted rationally for a change, it would help."

Her head snapped up sharply at the angry tone. Brendon was lounging in a sidechair by the unlit fireplace. Wearing a dark blue suit, he had the weary look of a man who had come directly from the office after a long day. "It's not like you to run, Savannah," he said slowly, rising to his feet. "But then last night was pleasure, not business, so maybe I should have expected it."

She wet suddenly dry lips and raked her teeth across her lower lip. "Why did you run out on me this morning?" he demanded softly. "What scares you so about working with me?" He moved to her side and ran his hands caressingly from her elbow to her shoulders.

She shrugged free of his seductive grasp. She was frightened of the power he had over her, afraid of the love she felt for him. "I'm not scared," she said.

He stalked her relentlessly, giving her only the barest physical inch. "You've never been so emotionally and physically involved with a man, have you? Last night—"

"Was a mistake." His nearness was clouding her judgment, making it difficult for her to think.

Brendon stared out the window toward Emerson's mansion for a long, tension-filled moment. "Is that why you were calling around town today, checking into other construction firms?"

She grimaced. Knowing Charleston's business grapevine, she should have expected he would hear about that.

He reached into his pocket and withdrew a sheaf of documents. "I suggest you read these before searching further." She glanced at him inquiringly as he continued. "It's a court injunction, Savannah, preventing McLean Development from implementing any of my suggestions at Paradise without Sloane Construction's participation in the project."

She paled. "When did you do this?" Her throat was achingly dry. Shock warred with the thought that she'd been betrayed.

"Earlier today." He faced her grimly. "I've got witnesses at the construction site who will verify that we've been collaborating on the project. There's also my meeting at McLean yesterday with Emerson. It wasn't difficult to get a judge to order that all work be stopped if we can't agree on how to proceed."

She swallowed. "An action like this could ruin my company, Brendon." Not to mention what it would do to her standing in the business community.

"Without the work, my firm will suffer a serious loss." He faced her equably.

She sat down, wondering how he could betray her so completely and still be so calm. "Does Emerson know about this?" she asked quietly.

"If he doesn't, he will soon."

Her temper flared out of control. "How could you do this to me?"

"I wanted to get the matter settled so we could go on."

"You're crazy if you think I'd make love with you after this!" She jumped to her feet and shoved the documents at him. Hot, angry tears blinded her eyes.

He tossed the documents aside and caught her against him. "I'm just protecting my interests, Savannah. And believe it or not, yours too."

"Get out!"

"Is that really what you want?" he asked in a soft, low tone.

Her breath came rapidly. She stared up into the glittering depths of his eyes, reading his intention before he moved. "No," she said, beginning to struggle anew. "I'm much too involved with you as it is!" But his lips were already grazing her parted lips. Her knees weakened traitorously despite the heated protests in her mind. "Stop," she pleaded against his hot mouth.

"If I thought you meant it, I would." His arms still clasped firmly around her waist, he moved her backward toward the couch, paying no attention to her resistance as he edged her knees against the plush upholstery. She toppled onto the throw pillows, his strong arms cushioning her fall, his prone length over hers accentuating her captivity.

"Brendon . . ." she warned furiously. Could he feel the pounding of her heart? Did he realize how much, despite everything, she wanted him to kiss her and make her forget everything but his touch, their love?

"Stop talking." His lips flitted over hers. She twisted her head, fighting to regain control. She pushed her back and shoulders further over the pillow-cushioned armrest. Brendon moved with her. The new position arched her even more intimately against him. He took advantage of the exposed line of her neck and pressed his face into her hair. The tip of his tongue traced the racing beat of her pulse.

"Let me go," she ordered huskily. But the hands that had been pushing against his chest now went almost obligingly around his neck.

Brendon kissed his way along the stubborn set of her jaw. Gently he nipped at her mouth while his hands traversed her lingeringly from waist to thigh. "Believe me, there are times, Savannah McLean, when I wish it were just that simple. But it isn't."

She shifted restlessly beneath him. Why did this Yankee charmer have such an inviting mouth? Why did he kiss so well, know just how to bring her to achingly wonderful heights? Why was she such easy prey? This feeling of being swept away hadn't happened with any other man. It was impossible not to think of making love with him again when the evidence of his desire was pressed so intimately against her, when his hands roamed her body so ardently.

"You want me," Brendon whispered persuasively, pausing to kiss her thoroughly again. Nimbly he dispensed with the black silk bowtie at her neck and unfastened the first three buttons of her blouse. "And God knows I want you."

"Brendon . . ."

"Damn it, Savannah, I want you in my life." He stopped and stared down at her. His voice shook slightly. "Why must you fight it so?"

"Because this attraction between us isn't going to last," she said. It would fade, the way the love in her marriage had faded. Only this time she didn't know if she could go on without him.

Heedlessly he parted her blouse, revealing a blue camisole. "Passion like ours doesn't die," he soothed softly, tracing the swell of her breasts above the lace. His knuckles brushed the tips until they tautened. She moaned, twisting beneath him, fighting herself more than him.

"I'll always want you, Savannah," he murmured more softly. "And you're always going to need me, whether you admit it or not."

Need, want: they were words far short of the love she was after. But as his fingers brushed aside the straps of her camisole to expose her creamy breasts to his ardent gaze, her ability to think faded. When his lips closed over one budding peak, she ceased resisting altogether and instead cradled his head more closely to her.

"You're so soft," he said, working the same magic over the twin peak. "So responsive." His teeth, lips, and tongue teased her to an aching frenzy. His hands spanned her waist and slid down over her hips to her skirt. Warm fingers eased beneath the hem to her knee. He robbed her of breath and will as his palm moved with tantalizing slowness up the inside of one thigh. When he reached the barrier of pantyhose and lace panties, his hand encountered the moist evidence of her desire. "Now tell me you don't want me," he said quietly, "and I'll go."

She started with shock as his palm slid away. He drew back slightly, propping the bulk of his weight on one bent elbow. His spine was pressed against the back of the sofa, his body at a right angle to hers. "I want the truth, Savannah," he commanded quietly, cutting off her sharp retort. "No more pretenses between us. No more evasions."

She glanced away furiously, fighting for whatever control and pride she had left. "Yes, I want you," she admitted tautly. But she didn't want to be used, sexually or professionally. She couldn't forgive him for getting the court order against her firm.

She slid from beneath him and straightened her blouse with trembling hands. Before he was on his feet again, she had flung open the door. "I also want you to go. And this time"—she yanked the engagement ring from her left hand—"take this atrocity with you!"

"Not fancy enough, hm?" Brendon stared at the solitaire dangling from her finger and thumb. He leaned forward to kiss her, but she turned her head. His mouth grazed her cheek instead. The warmth of the caress sent another fiery tingle shooting to her abdomen. Her knees were weak; her face flamed passionately.

"I'll see what I can do about adding a garnet and sapphires to your engagement ring," he said, recalling her earlier outrageous specifications. "But in the meantime you'll have to keep the ring. After all, we do need some evidence that we're still involved. And unless you're willing to go to Emerson now and confess the hoax as well as inform him of court orders..."

She wasn't. "Damn you!" She slammed the door after him. He laughed all the way to his car. Her ears were still hearing the sound as she studied the court injunction he had left behind.

"The sooner this problem is resolved the better," Emerson decreed to Savannah and John Crawford over coffee the next morning. "I don't want the courts involved in our dispute with Sloane Construction."

The conference room was littered with blueprints, computer printouts, and updated price lists. "Personally, I like Sloane's ideas for the upgraded interiors of the condominiums," John admitted, shrugging. "The experience of our sales force has shown that it's much easier to sell property built with all the extras than to convince the buyer to add them after the purchase. First, it's inconvenient to have workmen tromping through your home after you move in. Second, most customers have all they can handle financially just meeting the costs of moving and closing."

"We don't have any alternative when it comes to any of the subcontracting, either," Savannah admitted, sighing wearily and tossing down her pen. "So I guess we do business with Sloane. I'll have our legal department draw up the contracts right away. I know Brendon wants to get started as soon as possible."

The meeting adjourned. "Something else troubling you?" Emerson asked when John Crawford had left.

She glanced down at the ring on her hand. Much as she wanted to, she hadn't the courage to confess. "Nothing I can't handle, Grandfather." She leaned forward to kiss his cheek. "Thanks for being so understanding about this dispute with Sloane Construction." He'd been showing more forgiveness toward Brendon than she felt.

"Nonsense, Savannah. In Brendon's place, I would have done the same thing. And he's right—we do owe him, maybe for buying the property out from beneath him as well. At any rate, the project will be a success, it will be finished on time, and I'll retire knowing I'm leaving the company in good hands." He patted her shoulder. "Remember, this isn't our first dispute with Sloane, and frankly I doubt it will be our last. We just have to learn to work these problems out and go on."

Easier said than done, Savannah thought.

Savannah spent the next two days working on the Paradise project. Brendon called several times, but she ignored his messages and neglected to return his calls. She was still angry with him for the court order, and she needed to hold on to her anger. It was the easiest way to keep him and her turbulent emotions at bay.

On the afternoon of the third day she drove out to Edisto Island, where a professional photographer and four models waited for her. A girl and a boy pretended to play near carefully sculpted sand castles on the shore. The "father" and "mother" strolled hand in hand down the private wind-swept beach, then posed in several casually loving attitudes. "Kind of makes you yearn for the good old American dream, doesn't it?" a low male voice whispered in her ear.

She started abruptly from her reverie and turned to face Brendon. She'd dressed for work in a tailored suit and silk shirt. Brendon, on the other hand, looked ruggedly fit in khaki trousers, construction-style boots, preppy navy khaki and white tattersal shirt, and soft down vest.

"What are you doing here?" After what he had put her through, she felt it wise to keep all her defenses intact. It wasn't easy with her heart doing a machine-gun tap dance against her ribs.

"Watching the photographers, at least momentarily. Are you preparing promotional material?"

She nodded stiffly, hating his casual smile. "We'll select a couple of different shots by the end of the week which will appear in all the resort literature in March, April, and May magazines. The travel agencies in the area as well as along the Atlantic coast will have copies of our brochures. I hope, the ads and beachside copy alone will generate a lot of interest."

Brendon nodded. "It's going to be a beautiful place to retire." He fixed her with a steady, sensual gaze. "Or raise a family."

"Don't you have something to do?" she asked, turning to watch the photographer arrange all four models on a blanket spread with a picnic lunch. A dog, also employed, wouldn't cooperate and kept running after the beach ball. Savannah laughed as the frisky canine dashed unexpectedly into the surf, and returned to shake the saltwater onto the four people on the blanket. Screams and curses split the air.

Brendon took her firmly by the elbow and led her off to the side. "I want to take you to dinner," he said softly.

She glanced back at the models, who were still in disarray. "I don't think so, Brendon." She evaded his searching gaze. She'd been hurt enough already.

"Please, Savannah." His hand was around hers, his fingers covering the diamond she still wore, however reluctantly. "Let me make up for the other night. I know I was out of line."

"Do you?" she asked, her voice cool with disbelief. He had seemed awfully sure of himself.

"I wanted you. I thought you wanted me, too. It hurt me when you denied what you felt," he said simply.

"Brendon . . ." Her throat tightened with emotion. Love, want, need—her relationship with him had turned her life upside down. He had hindered her professionally, and if her grandfather had been less understanding, Brendon might have cost her her job. He offered no future other than a continuing affair, and she was beginning to realize she wasn't cut out for love on the sly.

"I won't pressure you, Savannah," Brendon said quietly. "I promise. Just have dinner with me."

But could she trust herself? One touch, one kiss, and she was his for the asking.

"We're going to be working together," he pointed out. "It only makes sense to be civil."

His tone was so presumptuous that her blood boiled. She pulled away from him abruptly. "I will be courteous to you, but I don't have to climb into your bed. I'll see you at work, Brendon, and we'll be friends. But that's all."

His brows rose. "I wasn't asking for a mercy mission of love, Savannah."

"Good!" she retorted, "because you wouldn't get one from me!"

He stroked his jaw lazily and favored her with a smile. "Only three nights ago you were—"

"I remember very well what I was doing!" she interrupted, enraged that he would behave so ill bred as to bring up her lack of judgment.

The corners of his mouth quirked humorously. "Want to do it again?"

"No!"

He gave her a mocking look When she glared back, he took a threatening step forward. "Perhaps the lady needs a lesson in passion and the inability of most humans to control it. That is, if you are human." He pretended to peer down the neckline of her blouse. "Maybe you even have a heart in there somewhere."

She was annoyed to feel herself blush. "The only thing I ever felt for you was lust, pure and simple!"

His hands clamped onto her shoulders. "The way I'm feeling now, that will do."

"Let go of me!" She tried to shrug free of his grip but failed. The photographers and crew had moved further down the beach.

"Gladly," Brendon said. "As soon as you come to your senses and stop all this nonsense and agree to have dinner with me."

"No." She tossed the hair from her eyes with a defiant shake of her head.

"Breakfast then, tomorrow."

"Forget it!"

His grip on her tightened. "What are you afraid of, Savannah? It's clear that you're terrified of something."

She pushed past him. He moved with her, blocking her exit. "Just leave me alone!"

He crossed his arms over his chest. "I find that very hard to do. We're engaged, remember? If we don't see each other occasionally, people will talk."

"Let them."

"You may not care about your reputation, but I most assuredly care about mine."

"Ha!"

He laughed, then his voice lowered cajolingly. "Come on, sweetheart. Just one more dinner. That's all I ask."

She read the desire in his eyes, and it frightened her. If she made love with him again, she'd never be able to break their engagement. He would break her heart first.

"I'm sorry, Brendon," she stated coolly. "I can't and won't be a convenient outlet for your physical passion. I'll see you at work whenever necessary. I'll try to be pleasant, but don't expect any more than that from me."

He caught her in a steely grip before she could turn away. Her breath lodged in her throat as he studied her. "It's not that easy, Savannah."

"Isn't it?" she shot back haughtily, determined to show him just how independent she could be. "You can't force me to see you."

"Want to bet?" She started to speak again, but he cut her off with a voice laced with steel. "Ever heard of a breach-of-promise suit? I'd hate to bring one against you, but I will if you leave me no other choice."

She gulped, thinking how swiftly he'd managed to get the court injunction against her firm. But she faced him with a disdainful air. "Breach-of-promise suits are outmoded and difficult to prove."

"They also bring lots of publicity, and bad press is something neither of us can afford," he countered smoothly. "Think about it before you refuse to see me again."

Frustration burned inside her. "You'd force me to see you, knowing I'd detest you for it?" she asked, deeply hurt and amazed.

Brendon glanced impatiently away and sighed. "You don't detest me, Savannah. You never have and you never will. Oh, I make you angry all right—angry as hell. But that doesn't change the way you feel about me. If you're honest, you'll admit you don't want to give up our affair any more than I do."

Affair, passion, lust! That was all they shared. Whatever happened to good old-fashioned love and commitment? Whatever happened to marriage, she wondered angrily. "That's where you're wrong," she said quietly. He had forced her into a corner for the last time. "Because I'm going to Emerson right now and tell him what I've done, and there's nothing you can do to stop me."

His brows rose, but he released his grip on her. She strode rapidly away, afraid to look back, afraid he would see the tears of anger and frustration in her eyes.

Savannah left the construction site immediately and drove back into Charleston, her thoughts in turmoil. Brendon was right. She didn't want to stop seeing him. She loved him. But she couldn't go on living a lie. She had to tell Emerson the truth. After that... well, she wouldn't think about it now. She'd handle one man and one dilemma at a time.

She found Emerson at home in the drawing room, enjoying high tea. "All right, what's the matter?" he asked as soon as she sat down.

"It's this whole engagement," she blurted, removing her ring. "It was a farce from the beginning. It started out as a practical joke, just as you assumed, then got completely out of hand." Her grandfather listened expressionlessly as she miserably related the details. Finished, she covered her eyes with her palms. "I'm sorry, I really am."

"That's quite a story," he said finally.

"You don't seem very surprised." She stared at him in amazement. In fact, he was taking the news very well— too well.

Footsteps sounded on the parquet floor, and she turned to see Brendon standing in the doorway, still dressed in his construction-site garb. Tammy Jo hovered in the background. Surprised to see him, Savannah expected him to be angry after the argument they'd had and the threats he'd made, but he was as calm as her grandfather. He shut the doors behind him and strolled into the room.

"I've told my grandfather," Savannah admitted.

Brendon nodded and glanced at Emerson. Their eyes held; slowly the two men exchanged smiles. Resentment flowed through Savannah. What was going on between them?

"I've called a halt to the deception." She stood up, hoping to dismiss Brendon, facing him for what she hoped would be the very last time. "It's over," she said with finality.

He laughed. "Not quite," he corrected. "Aren't you forgetting the first rule of business?" Brendon continued lazily, his wrist closing over hers. "It's imperative that we both project stable personal and professional images, at least superficially. We can't get engaged one week and break it off the next and still expect to inspire confidence in the people who work for us."

Savannah remained silent, her heart pounding against her rib cage, her hands moist with perspiration. Her duties and responsibilities at McLean Development weighed heavily on her, but more important was her desire to break her false engagement to Brendon. "How much longer do you want this to go on?" she demanded impatiently.

"At the very least, until Paradise opens in April," Brendon stipulated. "After that—"

She cut him off briskly, rage flooding her. "You're being impossible!" She turned to Emerson, expecting him to back her up. But he raised both hands in surrender.

"Honey, this is one argument you and Brendon will have to settle yourselves. I can't help you."

"Brendon has threatened to sue me for breach of promise!" she blurted.

Emerson inclined his head toward the younger man. "Is that so?"

"I'm afraid it is." Brendon rubbed his jaw ruefully. Emerson laughed.

Savannah stared at them in exasperation. "What is this," she demanded, "men against the woman and I lose? I'm your granddaughter, for heaven's sake! Help me!"

"Just what do you want me to do?" Emerson asked over the top of his bifocals.

"Talk some sense into that man!" She pointed at Brendon.

"He seems to be doing just fine on his own," Emerson observed. "As a matter of fact, I like the way he thinks. Son, why don't you fix us all a drink? Savannah looks like she needs one."

"Gladly." Brendon strolled over to the bar, looking infuriatingly at home.

Savannah's thoughts veered in a thousand directions. She

wanted to run and hide until Brendon went away and her predicament was somehow miraculously resolved. But she knew she'd been procrastinating long enough. She had to face her feelings about Brendon and the engagement. She had to resolve the situation and get on with her life.

She turned back to her grandfather, determined to win his sympathy. "Will you please stop being so cordial to our guest and listen to me?" she demanded. "I understand if you're angry. You have every reason to be, considering the prank I pulled."

"I'm not angry with you." Emerson pulled a cigar from his inner coat pocket and calmly unwrapped it.

"Well, for heaven's sake, why aren't you angry with me, or at least a little upset?" Honestly, men could be so annoying. The two of them looked as if they'd been in cahoots for years . . . was that possible . . . ?

Brendon sighed. "I think she's catching on." He handed Emerson and Savannah each a small tumbler of bourbon and branch water. "Emerson has known we've been joshing him for some time, Savannah. The fact that he didn't mention it was his way of joshing you back."

She swallowed in dismay. So all her vague suspicions had been right after all.

"But perhaps we'd better back up a bit," Brendon continued, collecting his own drink. He sat down on the sofa and drew her down beside him. "Emerson and I have had our differences during the past five years. The Paradise project was the last straw. It created a lot of ill will between our two firms. Several days before you and I met, Emerson and I got together at my urging and talked about the situation. We found we had a lot in common. He mentioned that you would eventually be taking over the firm and said he would like the two of us to meet. We arranged a rendezvous at the Mills House Hotel. The plan was that Emerson would introduce the subject of our meeting over lunch. At his signal I would casually drop by and say hello. Unfortunately, the two of you got into an argument soon after you arrived. The sign to meet you never came. When you finally stood up, I assumed you were leaving and that I had missed Emerson's signal while I was working on contracts. I followed you to the powder room, planning to introduce myself."

"I pretended to disapprove of Brendon as a practical joke," Emerson interjected. "After the argument we'd had about your dating, I knew you wouldn't be at all receptive to meeting someone."

Savannah sighed. What a fool she had been, and how easily they had duped her. "Your adamant reaction to Brendon did pique my curiosity," she admitted reluctantly. "I thought about the scene between you for the rest of the day. And then when I ran into Brendon that night at the Wine Cellar . . ."

"It was a setup," Brendon admitted. "Emerson phoned to apologize for his prank and explain. During the same conversation he hinted about where the two of you would be dining that evening. I wanted to see you again, Savannah. I offered to take his place."

Emerson shrugged. "I really did have a meeting with the school board that evening."

She glared resentfully at him. "Still, fixing me up as if I were a—a—"

"Beautiful young woman on the rebound," Emerson finished softly. "I don't regret it, Savannah. And apparently neither does your beau."

"Of course you surprised us both with your next move," Brendon continued. "When you came to my office that day, I didn't know what to think. But again, the chance to play a practical joke on Emerson was too good to resist. I upped the stakes and mentioned marriage to convince him we really were serious. And also, of course, to play a practical joke on you, Savannah."

She groaned aloud and buried her face in her hands. "I don't believe this," she moaned.

"I'm also a businessman," Brendon added. "When I saw the chance to recoup some of my initial loss on Paradise, I took it."

She looked at her grandfather. "And you don't hold that against him?" she asked incredulously.

Emerson shook his head and took another sip of his drink. "If I'd been in his place, I would have done the same thing."

"What about the party?" she asked. "If you knew our engagment was a hoax, why did you give us your public blessing?"

Emerson sighed. "Because by then, I really was confused. I didn't know whether it was a joke or not. And when I walked up to your carriage house that morning and saw the two of you together . . . suffice it to say I remember all too well what it was like to be falling in love. The party was my way of protecting your reputation and ensuring that Brendon's intentions toward you were honorable. It also finally laid to rest rumors about the dissension between our two firms. And it introduced Brendon to proper society in a very formal way, which is something that should have been done long ago."

Savannah cradled the icy glass between her palms. "Was your offer of the presidency a joke, too?" she asked, disappointment lacing her tone.

Emerson smiled indulgently at her. "Honey, I made up my mind to give you the position the day we last argued about it in my office. I knew at the time I was being unfair to you and, much as it pains me to admit it, chauvinistic, too. You'd done a heck of a job revamping the Paradise project and had more than proved your dedication to the firm. I was very proud of you. Unfortunately, before I had a chance to tell you I had changed my mind, you showed up with Brendon. The chance to pay you back with a little of your own medicine was very tempting."

"So you never meant to hold me to the engagement." She sighed, greatly relieved.

"No, I knew as soon as you came to me that if you did, I would reverse the decision. The presidency is yours, Savannah. I've already talked to the board of directors, and they've given you the okay. Crawford is quite content with his position as company vice-president." Emerson rose. "Now if the two of you will excuse me, I'm going to meet some cronies for a high-stakes poker game." He kissed Savannah and shook Brendon's hand, then left the room.

"We need to talk," Brendon said the moment they were alone.

"Not today." Too much had happened. Savannah couldn't take it all in or begin to sort her feelings. She left the room, walked briskly through the front door and down the steps toward the carriage house. Brendon was right behind her. "You can't come in," she informed him as she dug for her keys.

Anger smoldered in his eyes. "I see. Now that you've won the presidency and have no further need of my services, I can be on my way."

Embarrassment heated her face. "Are you implying *I've* used you?" What a hoot, considering how much social mileage he'd gotten out of their engagement!

"You're certainly building a good case," he responded grimly.

She recalled the last time he'd been in her carriage house and the court injunction he had brought. "Still planning to sue me for breach of promise?" she asked, unlocking the door and marching inside. Whirling, she faced Brendon. Unable to admit how vulnerable she felt with him, she said angrily, "If you have the paperwork with you, we could go over it, maybe even figure out exactly how much of a financial settlement a broken heart entitles you to. What would you like in payment, Brendon? My house? The ring?" In her agitation she could not pull it off her finger. How could he have betrayed her so mercilessly? Pain twisted inside her.

"Cut it out, Savannah." Brendon stepped inside and shut the door behind him. "You know I didn't mean that."

"Do I?" She faced him coldly, hooking her hands over the back of a chair for support. Her legs were trembling, and she was treacherously close to tears.

Striding nearer, he ignored her sarcasm. The room was bathed in shadows and smoky gray light. "Yes, you do, damn it," he said softly. "I've never tried to hurt you."

"But you didn't mind making a fool of me, did you?"

"I never made a fool of you, Savannah," he said quietly. "Everything I've felt for you has been very real."

Looking at him, she could almost believe him. "Then why did you push me into the engagement?" she asked, her rage fading. "Why did you insist on buying this ring? Why, even now, won't you let me go?"

"Because I want you with me, now and forever." He took her into his arms. His breath was warm against her cheek. "You've been pushing me away, and it scares me." He stroked her back with light, comforting motions. "I don't want to lose the closeness we've found. I don't think you do, either. But I'm tired of playing games. I want our engagement to end."

She pushed against him, but he held onto her, his arms lightly but firmly encircling her waist. Her feeling of loss was overwhelming. She hadn't expected him to want to leave her completely.

"I want to elope," he continued gently, persuasively.

"What?" She stared at him in amazement.

"You heard me," he repeated softly. "I want to elope." He slid his hand under her jacket. His palm splayed possessively across her back as he drew her near. "We're good for each other, Savannah." He stroked her spine, making warmth radiate through her silk blouse. "We're compatible in bed. We work the same long hours. We're in the same business, and we're both committed to our jobs. I admire your success and cherish you as a woman." He recited the reasons calmly, persuasively. His free hand moved up to touch her face in a tender gesture.

"Brendon, be serious." She stared at him, a tight knot of emotion closing her throat. A proposal was what she'd always wanted from him, but now that he'd given it, she found she couldn't believe him. She didn't completely trust him. More important, she didn't trust herself. "We haven't known each other long enough. It's only been a week."

He cupped a hand around her neck and lifted her chin. His lips grazed hers lightly. "I don't care how long it's been. I'm thirty-three years old and I never felt so wonderful. I know everything I need to know about you. You're beautiful, intelligent, and most important, you're not afraid to fight with me if I get out of line. You have a terrible temper and a quick tongue and a streak of impetuousness a mile wide. And none of it detracts in any way. I want you with me, Savannah. I want us to be married."

She stared at him, certain he'd lost his mind or was— perish the thought—playing another horrible joke! "You're just doing this because of the engagment," she asserted. "Out of some misguided sense of honor or—or chivalry."

He laughed. "That'll be the day! You ought to know by now that I don't give a damn what people think. That's why it's taken me so long to be accepted in this town. I don't give a damn about decorum. But you do, and I'm tired of seeing you hurt and embarrassed. I want to be able to love you any time of the night or day. I want you to feel good about us."

Part of her wanted that, too. Oh so very much. But suddenly she was afraid. She'd been hurt before, and it would be so much worse to be hurt by Brendon.

"I love you, Savannah," he said quietly.

"I love you, too." Tears of elation and despair burned in her eyes. She pulled away from him and wandered rest- lessly about the room, already feeling trapped. "But you've never been married. It's not all fun and games."

"And the last week has been?" he asked with a ghost of a grin.

"It's been a lot more fun than marriage. Believe me, Brendon, you'd be tired of me as soon as you got the ring on my finger."

"I'll never be tired of you." He tried to take her into his arms, but she pushed him away.

"You're probably right," she agreed nervously. "At first it wouldn't be so bad. But then boredom would set in and we'd have to deal with the dishes and the laundry and who forgot to pick up the dry cleaning. The next thing you know, major battle lines would be drawn and we'd be yelling and hating and hurting. I don't want that for us, Brendon. I couldn't bear it."

"Doesn't our love count for anything?" he asked softly.

Fresh tears burned behind her eyelids, but she refused to let them fall. "Of course it counts. It's just that love fades when people are together day in and day out."

"That won't happen to us, I promise."

"You're so naive." Desperately she wanted him to understand what she had learned in the most bitter of life experiences. "Before I married I had exactly the same rosy picture you do now. Take my word for it, it doesn't work that way."

"Then what do you suggest we do?" he queried tightly. "Live together? Do you want me to sneak in and out of your carriage house like a thief in the night? Do you want us to pack a suitcase and toothbrush every time we want to spend a few moments together? Do we keep checking into motels as Mr. and Mrs. Washington Carver?"

"It isn't funny!" she shouted back. He was treating her like a child!

"I'm not good enough for you, am I?" he said tensely after a moment. "Is my blood lacking in aristocratic genes? Do I embarrass you at country-club parties?"

"Don't be ridiculous!" she retorted. "I had a wonderful time at that party." Her voice lowered. "The best time I've had in years."

"Then marry me."

"I can't. You'd end up hating me. I remember when Keith and my car broke down on the San Diego freeway during rush hour because I forgot to check the water and the oil. There was smoke all over the place, the car almost caught fire, and Keith was swearing and screaming my name." She choked back the memories along with her guilt and misery.

"If the car breaks down, I won't swear at you," he said softly.

She stared at him suspiciously. "How can you be so sure?" Didn't he understand any of what she was trying to tell him?

"Do you trust me so little?" A muscle worked in his cheek.

"That's just it—I don't know. Nobody does until after it's too late. How would I know how you'd react when the car breaks down?"

"How indeed," he murmured with an exasperated sigh.

"Look, it's not you I'm doubting," she hastened to assure him. "It's me, it's everything, it's—"

"Marriage," he finished grimly. He took a deep breath. "What if we prolong our engagement to give you time to get used to the idea?"

Her doubts resurfaced. "To be perfectly honest, I don't think it would make any difference," she confessed wearily. "When I divorced I promised myself I would never marry again." Experience told her she'd be a fool to break that vow now.

"I see." He straightened lazily and ran a hand through his hair. "Don't date anyone else, Savannah. Don't even think about it. I'll call you in a few days, after you've had time to think." He left, closing the door very carefully behind him. She stared at it for long moments afterward. Never had she felt more of a fool. But that tight knot of apprehension buried deep inside her just wouldn't go away.

CHAPTER
Fourteen

"WELL, WHAT DO you think?" Brendon asked Savannah three days later as they toured the twenty-five-hundred-square-foot structure that would be the sales office and information center at Paradise. The concrete floor was uncarpeted. Huge beams of both stained ash and rough cedar had been deposited in the center of the sawdust covered floor.

She shivered in her raincoat. She wore a silky beige shirtdress and white cashmere blazer, neither of which offered much protection against Brendon's raking glance. She felt as vulnerable as if she were naked. "I prefer the stained ash," she said, "but some people like the rustic look. I think we should use the stained ash in the information center, but alternate the use of cedar and ash throughout the various models."

"My feelings exactly," Brendon agreed with a pleasant grin.

She warmed to his smile but pinned him with a steady look. True to his word, he'd given her plenty of time to think. But, though her fears had abated, they hadn't disappeared entirely. She kept wondering how he'd react in the throes of a domestic crisis. She worried about her own ability to balance work and pleasure and still be everything a wife should be, everything that Brendon would want her to be. She worried that in the end she wouldn't be able to satisfy him.

Their business finished, they left the building. A chilly wind was blowing off the Atlantic. Brendon glanced up at the darkening sky. "We'd better get a move on. It looks like rain."

The construction site was devoid of workers. Savannah nodded and turned up her collar against the chill. "You're right. It does look bad. Another winter storm, I wonder?"

They were walking to her Seville. Brendon stopped unexpectedly and stared toward the complex entrance. Following his gaze, she stared aghast. A Sloane Construction bulldozer was neatly barring the only paved exit.

"Now what?" She stared at him dispiritedly. It would be dark soon. Apparently everyone else had gone home for the day.

"Let's hope there's a key in it." Brendon strode over to the bulldozer, his coattails flapping in the wind. He wore a three-piece wool suit, striped shirt, and silvery gray tie, with no overcoat. Savannah slid behind the driver's seat of her car and watched as he climbed up onto the huge machine. A moment later he was hopping back down again. His face was grim as he headed toward her.

"Can't you move it?" she asked.

"There aren't any keys."

With effort she stifled a sharp remark about his company's incompetence. He opened the door on the driver's side. "Move over, sweetheart. There's a back way out of here, but it's not the easiest to manuever. You'd better let me drive."

"No deal. I drove us out here. I'll drive us back."

Brendon's mouth tightened. For a moment she thought

he would physically shift her into the passenger seat. Muttering words she didn't want to decipher, he shut her door, strode around the front of the car, and got in on the passenger side stiffly but quietly.

Her own temper raging, she stared straight ahead. This was precisely the way Keith would have reacted. True, her ex-husband would have been more virulent in his disagreement, but she and Brendon weren't married yet, either. No doubt he was on his very best "courtship" behavior. A little devil prodded her to push him just a bit further. If he were prone to excessive criticism or temperament, what better way to find out?

Brendon fastened his seatbelt and leaned back against the seat. "Go forward about one hundred feet and turn right," he directed. "There's a muddy jeep trail that's been strewn loosely with gravel. You'll have to go slowly and be careful, but I think you can make it."

"How nice for the vote of confidence," Savannah noted sarcastically. He glanced at her quizzically, then turned back to the road with a shrug.

She drove with deliberate slowness. Brendon sighed his irritation. "I'm just being careful," she said.

"It will be dark soon. There aren't any overhead lights."

He had a point. "Oh, all right." She pressed down on the accelerator, and the car shot ahead. She eased up on the pedal, and it jerked back.

Brendon frowned, glancing worriedly at the mud on either side of the trail. "Watch what you're doing," he said quietly.

"I was." Darn him for rebuking her anyway!

"Would you like me to drive?" he offered.

"No." More angry with herself than him, she pressed again on the accelerator. The sooner they got home, the better.

"You're going to have to turn right up here," he cautioned.

"I see the turnoff," she shot back. Keith had always snapped out directions when she drove. The resulting tension and anger had only made her more reckless. She was dismayed to find that her instinctive reaction hadn't changed.

"Slow down!" Brendon put his hands up over his face as if to ward off an impending crash.

I am!" She stomped on the brake, simultaneously jerking the wheel hard to the right. She could have handled the stop, turn, and start, but she hadn't anticipated the slick mud and a patch of gravelless ground. The car slid sideways, barely missing a truckload of bricks, then fishtailed hard. Her hands gripped the wheel and held. Her foot pressed the brake pedal as far as it would go. Seconds later she realized the car had halted. She clutched the steering wheel tremulously, her heart pounding in her chest.

Brendon smiled. "Way to go, hotshot," he observed. "Still feel inclined to show off?" She muttered something he couldn't understand. He ignored her. "Just straighten the car around and let's get out of here."

Sobered into good behavior despite his goading remarks, she sat up straight and took a deep, steadying breath. Mentally prepared, she pressed down lightly on the accelerator. The car wheels spun with a grinding noise, slanted toward the load of bricks, then down. "Oh, this is even better," Brendon observed cheerily as he glanced out the passenger window. "We're sinking."

Hot, angry tears pricked her eyes. She felt like such a fool. He shook his head in exasperation. "I'll see how bad it is."

The car door slammed. She closed her eyes and leaned her head against the steering wheel. When Brendon returned, his beautiful suit trousers and expensive leather shoes were covered with mud. "It's bad, but I think I can get us out," he said grimly. "Do you want to let me drive now or would you prefer to risk getting us in deeper? I will caution you, there are no phone lines out here yet, and although I do have a shortwave radio, it's in my company jeep, which we left back in Charleston, at your insistence."

Thoroughly ashamed for overreacting, she reached for the door handle on her side. "You drive," she said quietly.

"No, don't, I'll get out." He placed a restraining hand on her arm, and his tone was protectively tender. "I'm already muddy."

They changed places. Adeptly he steered the car out of the mud. It was a miracle they hadn't gotten stuck, and Savannah said a silent prayer of thanks as Brendon drove slowly out of the construction complex. Daylight faded as they turned onto a gravel road through the marsh. "Where will this take us?" she asked. She'd only been in and out of the complex via the main entrance.

Brendon shook his head. "I wish I knew. We're heading west. You wouldn't happen to have a map, would you?"

She extracted one from the glove compartment. "Well?" he inquired after a moment.

"I'm looking, I'm looking." But it was impossible to read the tiny letters with the car bumping and jolting. "We seem to be in the middle of a marsh," she finally said. "About a mile or two from the Atlantic Ocean."

"That much I knew." He grinned, appearing not the least bit upset. He halted the car and suggested pleasantly, "Why don't we look at it together?"

There was no doubt about it, he was a good sport. She was quiet as he calmly studied the map. The headlights of her car illuminated a trail through the marshy land. Grass at least six feet tall grew on either side of the gravel road. Actually it was rather spooky out here. She was glad Brendon was with her.

He glanced around thoughtfully. "I think I know where we are."

She breathed an enormous sigh of relief.

Without warning the car sputtered and choked. Terrified, she glanced at Brendon. How long since she'd had the oil or water checked? "We're not going to get stuck out here, are we?" she asked, a nervous quaver in her voice.

He shot her a faintly amused glance. "Afraid the ghosties and goblins will get you?"

She swallowed but couldn't totally subdue her fear. She had never liked dark places. Before she could reply, the car sputtered again, choked, and died. The head lights shined into empty darkness. "What's the matter?" she asked.

Brendon frowned. He stared at the dashboard, tried the ignition, then said calmly, "It would seem we are out of gas."

"Oh, no."

"Oh, yes." He removed the keys from the ignition and opened his door. "I think we'd better walk, unless you'd like to stay here all night."

"But we're lost," she exclaimed.

"Not really." He glanced up at the midnight blue sky. "Ever learn to read the constellations?"

She shook her head. "Pity." He sighed. "Neither did I." He held out his arm. "Shall we go?"

"We've been walking for hours," Savannah complained. The tall grass had become interspersed with trees as the terrain sloped upward, and the ocean seemed miles away.

"More like half an hour," he observed.

She peered at her watch. "One and a half."

He shrugged. "Sorry."

"I thought you said you knew where we were."

"I do, sort of. Highway Seventeen is north of us. The Edisto River borders us on the east. The Combahee River is due west."

"How far to the nearest town?" she asked.

"By my calculations, ten miles."

She groaned. Fatigue seemed to wrench at her every muscle.

"Don't worry," Brendon comforted, "there are homes out here. We should come across one soon. In fact..." he mused, coming unexpectedly to a halt.

Savannah turned in the direction of his gaze. Her eyes widened speculatively at the sight of a towering A-frame structure, but her brain refused to accept the image her gaze conveyed. "Are we hallucinating?" she asked.

Brendon rubbed his jaw. "If we are, I don't want to wake up."

She stared at the dark windows. "Too bad no one's home. We could have called the auto club."

He turned toward her with a careless shrug. "We still can. All we have to do is get to the phone."

"That's called breaking and entering," she informed him tartly. "It's a felony."

"Only if we get caught."

"Brendon!"

"I'm teasing. I'm sure the owners will understand," he persisted softly. "We own two of the best construction companies in the state. If we harm anything, we'll fix it. We'll build them a pool by way of compensation, if that's what they want."

She was tired and cold. She didn't want to break the law, but, try as she might, she didn't see any other houses or even lights. And there was no telling where that winding jeep trail would take them. "All right," she finally agreed. "But let's not break any glass unless we absolutely have to."

"Okay."

They walked to the door and rang the bell. Predictably, no one answered. "How do you plan to do this?" Savannah asked, half expecting at any moment to be shot or to set off a burglar alarm.

"Let's try a key." Brendon pulled a ring full of them from his pocket.

"The chances of even a master key working are nil," she said. But to her surprise, the door swung open on his second try. She stared at him, bemused. "I take it back. You *are* a genius."

"Thanks." He swung her up into his arms and carried her across the threshold, deposited her feet-first on the floor, shut the door, and flicked on a light. In the center of the beautifully decorated living room, a table had been set lavishly for two. Delicious aromas wafted from chafing dishes on the table. A bottle of champagne sat chilling in a bucket of ice.

"Someone's coming for dinner," Savannah said, looking frantically for a phone. "We'd better call the auto club and get out of here."

He laughed softly. "I have a confession to make. This is our house."

"Our house?" she echoed in confusion.

"I spent the last three days looking for a place where we could go to be alone. I wanted it close to the construction site, completely out of Charleston, and very private. I decided that if you didn't want to get married that was fine, but I still had to protect you from slanderous talk. I also wanted to be able to love you however and whenever the mood struck, without worrying about someone popping in."

She glanced at their luxurious surroundings. "You did all this for me?"

"I'd move heaven and earth if I thought it would make you happy. That's why I was so insistent that you accompany me to the site," he confessed softly. "I didn't plan on getting stuck in the mud or running out of gas or getting semilost. I did want to bring you here and propose all over again. If you still don't want marriage, I'll meet you on whatever terms are comfortable for you. I love you, Savannah. That's all that counts. You can have all the time you need."

Suddenly she didn't need any more time. Everything seemed to fall into place inside her. It felt thoroughly right to be there with Brendon as her previous fears and objections melted into thin air. Yes, she'd been hurt when her marriage to Keith failed. But Brendon was a very different man from Keith and, come to think of it, she'd changed a lot too in the last year. She had a better perspective on what she wanted from life—and she wanted Brendon. She would never love another man so deeply, so completely.

"I don't need any more time to decide." She bridged the distance between them and put her arms around his waist, brimming with happiness.

"What about all your doubts?" He put a gentle hand under her chin and lifted her face to his. "Are you still afraid marriage will ruin what we have?"

"I was until tonight," she admitted honestly.

"Does that mean you'll marry me?" he asked gently.

"Yes. First things first, though—I think we'd better get you out of those wet clothes."

He grinned and glanced down at his mud-caked suit pants. "Want to help?"

"Darling," Savannah purred, "I thought you'd never ask."

They walked arm in arm to the loft on the second floor, where a king-size bed dominated the room. She tossed off her raincoat and the blazer underneath. Brendon shrugged out of his suit coat and loosened his tie. She explored his broad shoulders, caressed the hard plane of his stomach, and struggled impatiently with his shirt buttons. He watched her, his eyes glowing passionately. His lips brushed her forehead affectionately as she tugged the fabric free of his pants. He groaned when she slid her fingertips under the waistband and touched his skin.

Her lips traced his, and he folded her closer. Her tongue plunged inside his mouth, only to withdraw and test the edges of his teeth. She nibbled at his lips. His hand pressed against her lower spine, forcing her closer still. She kissed him again, tasting, sipping, arousing. And then Brendon was invading her mouth, orchestrating the moves.

She watched as he took off his shirt. She started to shed her dress, but he stopped her with a cautioning finger. He traced a sensual swath into the neckline of her dress and the shadowy valley between her breasts. "Let me," he urged.

Slowly he unfastened the buttons and dispensed with the belt. The silly fabric slid from her arms. He pushed it over her hips and let it fall in a circle on the floor. Still gazing down at her, he grasped her bare arm and planted a trail of kisses from her wrist to her elbow. When he reached the tender underside of her arm, she moaned and shifted restlessly against him. "Patience, Savannah, I'm just starting," he teased, working equal havoc on her other arm.

"Brendon . . ." She didn't know if she'd be able to wait. She didn't know if she *wanted* to wait.

"You're a temptress, Savannah," he whispered, kissing his way back to her mouth. For long moments he bestowed his own brand of magic on her pliant lips. "Pure heaven. I've missed you the past few days."

"And I've missed you."

His caresses made her pulse speed crazily. Her heart pounded against her ribs as he peeled the half-slip from her hips. She shrugged out of it, enjoying his response almost as much as she loved the male-directed striptease. A flick of his fingers released the front clasp of her bra, letting her breasts tumble free. He cupped the curving flesh with both palms and gently kneaded the plump weight. He smiled as the nipples tautened.

"You're so sweet," he whispered against her mouth. "So good." His eyes burned into hers before he lowered his head. Her neck tilted back in abandon as his lips closed around her breast. He tugged lightly, rolling the taut flesh between his teeth, laving it with his tongue, soothing it with his lips. Each gentle touch sent a thousand new pinpricks of desire shooting through her. The knot of unslaked passion grew tighter, more demanding. She writhed against him, holding him close while at the same time wanting desperately, perversely, to push him away. "Brendon, I want you."

"I want you, too, sweetheart." Laughing together, they undressed swiftly. He was rigid with need, and the ache in her lower abdomen intensified. She was moist and warm and ready for him. "Savannah . . ."

"Please . . ."

"I love you."

"I love you, too." She loved him more than she had imagined loving any man. He moved her backward toward the bed. They kissed lingeringly and fell slowly onto the bedspread. His weight moved over her, and she welcomed him. He gazed at her tenderly, his arms supporting his weight. Reverently she ran her hands from his hips to his thighs. She covered his abdomen with her palms. She caressed his maleness and drew him closer to the moist softness of her flesh. They joined with a gasp of pleasure.

Brendon stilled momentarily. His hands trailed through her hair, then dropped to her breasts. He kissed her gently, then held her close and moved inside her, arching, thrusting, demanding, giving. She gripped his shoulders. Tears of passion covered her cheeks as they scaled the heights and drifted leisurely back to the present.

Brendon held her tightly, his face buried in her hair. His warm breath caressed her shoulder. The soothing motions of his hands gentled her. Utter contentment flowed through her as she relaxed against him. "Well?" he teased softly at last. "Still want to marry me, Ms. McLean?"

"More than ever." She nestled against his shoulder, loving his scent. "I meant it, though, when I said I was no superwoman. Sometimes my work is about all I can handle."

He propped his elbows on either side of the pillow and stared down at her. "I promise I'll be understanding. I'll also make sure there's plenty of gas in the tank."

She giggled. Her conscience made her add, "Ah, Brendon? I have a confession to make, too. I knew the car was low on gas."

"You didn't!" he accused, sitting bolt upright.

She blushed slightly. "I noticed after we left my office this afternoon. I figured I'd fill up on the way back to Charleston."

"Shame on you, woman." He shook his head in mock reproach and lay back down beside her. "I have a confession to make, too." He favored her with a sexy grin. "I noticed the tank was low long before we hit empty. After the way you'd behaved, I thought a little walk would do you good!"

She sat up abruptly. The sheet draped low over her breasts. "Are you telling the truth?"

He nodded. "I knew we'd show up at the house sooner or later. And frankly, if we could live through the past few hours, I think we can weather any crisis."

"True," she murmured, secretly pleased that his thoughts were as mischievous as hers often were. He was such a scoundrel, and she loved him madly.

"Come here and kiss me again," he insisted.

"With pleasure," she agreed, wrapping her arms around him and giving herself up to a kiss that expressed all the passion and love they would need in their lifetime together.

WATCH FOR
6 NEW TITLES EVERY MONTH!

Second Chance at Love

SK 41 a

67

WHAT READERS SAY ABOUT
SECOND CHANCE AT LOVE BOOKS

"I can't begin to thank you for the many, many hours of pure bliss I have received from the wonderful SECOND CHANCE [AT LOVE] books. Everyone I talk to lately has admitted their preference for SECOND CHANCE [AT LOVE] over all the other lines."
—*S. S., Phoenix, AZ**

"Hurrah for Berkley . . . the butterfly and its wonderful SECOND CHANCE AT LOVE."
—*G. B., Mount Prospect, IL**

"Thank you, thank you, thank you—I just had to write to let you know how much I love SECOND CHANCE AT LOVE . . . "
—*R. T., Abbeville, LA**

"It's so hard to wait 'til it's time for the next shipment . . . I hope your firm soon considers adding to the line."
—*P. D., Easton, PA**

"SECOND CHANCE AT LOVE is fantastic. I have been reading romances for as long as I can remember—and I enjoy SECOND CHANCE [AT LOVE] the best."
—*G. M., Quincy, IL**

*Names and addresses available upon request